ANGUS: COWBOY BEWILDERED

THE KAVANAGH BROTHERS BOOK 8

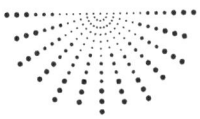

KATHLEEN BALL

Copyright © 2020 by Kathleen Ball

All rights reserved.

No part of this book may be reproduced in any form or by any electronic or mechanical means, including information storage and retrieval systems, without written permission from the author, except for the use of brief quotations in a book review.

❦ Created with Vellum

CHAPTER ONE

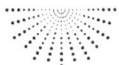

*A*ngus' hand twitched, ready to grab his gun.

For about a week now, he'd had the particular feeling he was being watched. Every time he turned, though, no one was there. His brothers enjoyed making fun of the "ghost" following him. A prickly sensation crept along his arms and up to his neck.

"Know-it-all, brothers," he muttered as he swept his gaze along the tree line. A branch moved, and he smiled. He'd catch his prey and prove he wasn't crazy.

Slowly he rounded up and pushed a few steers to the tree line monitoring the area where the tree stood. "Yaw!" He spurred Captain his paint on and drew his gun on the boy on a horse. He blinked.

A boy? Tarnation! He'd still be the mule's end of jokes.

The boy's brown eyes grew wide. "I-I wasn't spying. I was just l-learning is all," the boy stammered.

Angus holstered his gun. "Learning what?" He made sure his voice was extra gruff. This boy had to learn not to watch people. That kind of behavior would bring him harm someday.

The boy's bay sure had seen better days. It was an old horse with a swayed back. There was no saddle, but at least there was a bridle. The brown hat he wore was too big, as were his clothes. He'd rolled up his trousers and sleeves. Who *was* this boy?

"How to be a cowboy," the boy whispered. His gaze never wavered, and that impressed Angus.

"Where you from, boy?"

The boy swallowed hard. "Name is Julian Field, sir. I live on a ranch close to here. My pa is ill, and I work the ranch with him, but I wanted to be sure I was doing everything right. I work there most of the day and then head here to see what you're doing. I didn't mean any harm, sir."

"Name's Angus Kavanagh." He studied the boy. "You don't have any help over there? No one has worked that ranch in a long while. Is the barn still standing?"

"You know the place?"

Angus nodded. "More rock than pasture. What happened to your pa?"

Julian looked as though he'd missed too many meals.

"He was chopping wood and he got his leg sliced open. I took a needle to it and closed it up real good, but it's been smelling worse and worse. I'd best get back and check on him. He has fevers, some real bad." Julian glanced over his shoulder and started to turn the bay, but then he paused. "Sorry I watched you. I should have asked permission."

"I'll bring Sheila by this afternoon," called Angus. "She's a healer, she can help. I'll stop by in the morning and see what I can do to help too."

Julian's smile was bright. "Thank you, sir!"

"See you in the morning."

Julian aimed his horse for the woods and rode off, and after a few seconds, Angus turned Captain and rode for Sullivan's house to talk with Sheila, who was Sullivan's wife.

It sounded like maybe Julian and his pa could use all the help they could get.

Julian's heart was still beating hard when she returned home. Angus was much bigger up close. She'd learned a lot from watching him, but she wouldn't take the chance to do that again. She'd have to figure things out on her own.

First, though, she had to check on her father, and then she still had a couple more hours of ranch work to do. She tied her old bay horse to the hitching post, deep in thought. Would Sheila really come? Most times people said nice, hopeful things, but they didn't mean them. She hoped Angus meant the offer. As intimidating as he was, he did seem kind.

If he showed up in the morning, she'd give him a quick look at the ranch. He knew the place, he'd said, called it more rock than pasture; unfortunately, that was true. Perhaps he'd have a few suggestions to make the ranch better.

As she stepped through the door, she wrinkled her nose as her stomach pitched. The putrid smell in the cabin got worse by the day. There was hot water on the stove. It didn't seem to be helping, but she had to try something. After filling the basin, she grabbed a cloth and sat in the wooden chair next to her father's bed. She pulled up the sheet to expose his leg. As gently as she could, she washed his wound. His entire calf area was fiery red and though it wasn't bleeding, there was always yellow stuff dried on top of the stitches. She washed it off before it became dry if she could.

"Julian…" His voice was scratchy. "I can tell I'm done for. Listen to me. The deed is buried in a metal box under the back left corner of the house. There are papers of ownership for the animals. I love you. Perhaps I was wrong to allow you to grow up more cowboy than woman. Someday I hope you find love… I wish you to marry. Sell the cattle to pay for the taxes, then use the rest of the money for food. You know how." He coughed. His handsome face was now gaunt, and his eye sockets were prevalent.

"I know how, Pa." She kissed his forehead before she took the basin and threw the dirty water out the back. She needed to clean him up. There was only one clean sheet left. She'd be scrubbing sheets long into the night. He'd refused to allow her to get help. It was out of his hands now.

Lord, I'm pleading for healing for my father. I hope it's not his time. I'm not sure what will happen if he leaves me. Please hear my prayer, Lord.

A lone tear trailed down her face. It was hard work getting him cleaned and putting a fresh sheet beneath him. She tried to spoon broth into his mouth, but he only took about half of it. Cool water for his fever was next. She wiped down his arms and face before she left him to sleep.

As soon as she was outside, she made a fire near the well. Next, she put up the huge tripod and lifted the copper washtub onto the hook. It was easier to put the water into the pot near the well. Bucket after bucket she poured into it. Extra lye soap flakes went in and then the sheets from the last few days. They'd been soaking in cool water.

As strong as she was, just getting it all set up exhausted her. Then it was back into the house for her, Pa needed wiping down again. She grabbed the washboard on her way out. More water was needed for the tub. Women did this all the time. Why her back and shoulders hurt so puzzled her. And she still had the scrubbing to do.

By the time she was ready to hang the sheets on the line, the sun had passed midday. The sound of a buggy approaching truly surprised her. She had held out little hope. As it drew closer, she saw Angus and a woman she assumed was the healer, Sheila.

Thank You, Lord...

Angus stepped out of the buggy first and then hurried to the other side to help Sheila. He had amiable manners.

"Sheila, this is Julian," he introduced.

"It's nice to meet you, Julian." Sheila had such kind eyes. "Where is your father?"

"He's inside. Come." She expected some comment about the smell, but no one said a word about it. "Pa," she said, eliciting a moan. "Pa, these folks came to help." She looked at Sheila and Angus. "This is my pa, Jack Field."

Sheila sat on the wooden chair and pulled back the sheet. She nodded. Next, she took the wet cloth, wet it again before she laid it on his forehead. "I have some plants I need to grind. May I use your table?"

"Do you need help?" Julian offered.

Sheila stared at her for a moment then gave a gentle smile. "I'm fine in here. Angus can give you a hand with those sheets you're washing. I know it's backbreaking work."

ANGUS WANTED to ask how old Julian was, but he didn't want to insult the boy. His voice hadn't changed yet, and his face didn't need a razor. It was hard to tell his age, but he sure did a lot of work for a youngster.

They finished hanging the last clean sheet. Sheila hadn't come out to talk to Julian yet. Did that mean the news was grim? Angus had smelled the putrid smell of limbs dying in the war. That leg would probably have to come off.

"Julian, is there anything else you need doing tonight?"

Julian glanced at Angus with a surprised expression on his face. "I chop wood until I'm too tired to move and then fall into bed. The sun comes up and I'm at it again. It's hard work, but I want to make a go of this place. All my pa wanted was his own land. We were sharecroppers for as long as I can remember. But our share grew smaller each year. Finally, when it was just me and Pa, we left. So, I'm used to working from sunup to sundown." He shrugged his small shoulders then sent an anxious glance toward the cabin. "What do you think is happening?"

After trying to make his face expressionless, Angus caught Julian's gaze. "If anyone can help, it's Sheila. She knows about roots and plants. In fact, at one time she had to hide because people thought she was a witch. She's married to my brother Sullivan."

The boy's eyes grew wide. "A witch? What a sticky situation to be in."

Angus nodded. Julian was well educated for a sharecropper's child. All in all, he was impressive.

The door to the cabin opened, and Julian shoved his hands in his pockets, fixing a stoic expression on his face.

"He will need much care," Sheila announced with a sigh, "but I'm not willing to give up on him just yet. His fever has gone down a bit and I had to cut away a lot of dead and infected skin. Right now, I have a bandage around his leg. When you change it, it might be horrific to see. What you will see is uncovered muscle. I want the bandage changed twice a day and I left a bottle of oil I want you to rub onto the skin surrounding the wound. I left plenty of willow bark tea, but if the pain is too much, I'll need to bring laudanum."

"Why can't you leave some here?" Angus asked.

"Adults overdose on it, and I'm not comfortable allowing a younger person administer it." She smiled at Julian. "I'll stop by in a few days. I have a baby at home and can't be gone for too long."

"Leave the bottle," Angus said. "I'll stay and help around here. Then when you come, I can hold Lorna and watch Rachel too."

She sighed again and a smile spread across her face. "I can do that. I'll take the buggy home and send someone with clothes and things you'll need." She nodded.

Angus readied the buggy and Sheila climbed in and took the lines.

"This is genuinely nice of you, Angus." She waved to the two of them as she urged the horse forward.

He frowned. Wasn't he usually nice? She'd said it as though it was something out of the ordinary. His frown deepened as he watched her drive off.

CHAPTER TWO

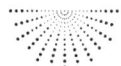

"If we move your father into the smaller bed, we can both have a piece of the bigger bed to get some shuteye," suggested Angus. "Don't worry, I have nine brothers and we've all shared at some point. I'm not sure how long I'll be here, but we might as well be comfortable." He stepped over to the smaller bed and took the comforter off. "Do you have clean sheets for this bed?"

She nodded. "I can do it."

"Honestly, you look as though you're about to fall over. Where are the sheets?"

Julian pointed under the bed. "There is a crate full of them. But I'm fine, really."

"After we move your pa, I want you to get to bed. I'm a light sleeper and I'll hear if your pa needs us." Angus got on his knees and looked under the bed. He pulled out the crate, picked up the sheet on top, and quickly made the bed. After he smoothed the last wrinkle, he turned to Julian. "Help me move him."

Her pa was like dead weight. They took hold of the corners of the cloth he was on and carried him. He screamed from the pain and she felt his cries go right through her. It was too much, and her eyes grew wet. She lowered her gaze, trying to hide her tears.

Once they got him onto the bed, she made him as comfortable as possible. "You'll be fine, Pa. We have help now, so I don't want you to worry about a thing." The brightness of his eyes concerned her. His forehead wasn't nearly as hot as earlier in the day, but he was still in a lot of pain.

"Angus, what about the laudanum? Could you give him some?" she practically pleaded.

Angus gave her a long look. "Sure, let me get it. I should have given it to him before we moved him. I'm sorry."

Angus administered the laudanum by mixing it in water and having her father drink it. "I think hunting might be on the list soon," he said as he tidied up.

"I've been trying as hard as I know. I can shoot, but I don't have great aim. I wish I could have done better." She sighed. Looking at the large bed, her heart pounded, and her mouth grew dry. "It might be best if I sleep on the floor."

"No need as long as you don't kick me all night." Angus grinned.

"I *am* a known kicker—"

He shot her an easy grin. "Get some sleep. I'll pick up a bit."

She wanted to protest, but what if he grew suspicious? Maybe she'd best sleep in her clothes. She took off her boots and got into bed. She had her back to him and held on to the edge of the mattress.

Lord, I don't know what to do. If I tell him the truth, he's bound to leave. I have to do what's necessary for my pa. Please bring Pa's health back. I need him. Don't let his time with me be over. Forgive me for pretending to be a boy. It's not honest, but I don't know what else to do. Almighty God, I beseech You to help me. Hear my prayer, Lord. Amen.

She closed her eyes and listened to each sound Angus made. Finally, the bed dipped, and his boots dropped. She almost screeched when she heard him undress. *He'd better have a union suit on.* The mattress bounced some and then it sounded like he flopped onto his back. Soon his loud snores filled the room.

After a near sleepless night, the first gray light of dawn filtered into the cabin. Julian slowly snuck out of bed and went to check on her pa. How was she going to change his bandage? It had been all she could do to sew him up. She'd been so sick afterward. She was used to the blood of butchering, but this was vastly different.

His head wasn't nearly as fiery as yesterday, though, so things were looking better. She lifted his head to see if she could get him to take more water.

His eyes flickered, and he gave her a small smile. "Hi sweetheart." He drank a swallow before she gently put his head back on the pillow.

"Pa," she whispered. "They think I'm a boy. I think it will keep me safe, just like before."

"You always were smart. I'll try to remember." He groaned. "Who is that man?"

"Angus Kavanagh. He brought his sister-in-law here yesterday. She's a healer, and Angus said he'll help me with the ranch."

He nodded. "Good, good. It's not right… the bed."

"Pa, I will be safe. Don't fuss. Do you think you could eat?"

"If there is any bread? I might like a hunk." The pain on his face tore at her. He looked to be anguished by each breath he took.

While her back was turned, Angus dressed, and she was forever grateful she didn't see a thing. Did she still look boyish enough? Everything had happened so quickly with

Angus and Sheila. She hadn't expected him to stay, so she'd had no time to prepare. The mirror on the wall didn't tell her much. Her hair was much shorter than a girl's and without it combed it reminded her of a scarecrow. Her face was red from the sun and her lips were chapped. Her body was more like a boy's too. She wasn't curvy at all. She was simply fine-boned with a thin boy body.

"Angus, after we eat, do you want to change the bandage? I can do it, but well…I can stand blood but not on someone I care about." Let Angus think her weak. Hopefully, he'd simply see it as a sign of immaturity.

Angus frowned. "What did you do before we bandaged him?"

"It wasn't easy and obviously I'm not good at healing." She stared at her boots. "If you must know, I was sick and had to run out of the cabin a time or two."

"Glad to help. I get the same way when a woman is in labor." Angus' face turned a slight shade of red.

"Lots of babies at the ranch?" she asked while she put a skillet on the stove.

"Every time I turn around there's more." He came beside her and sliced the bacon.

"So, it's not something you'd want? Babies, that is?" She needed to change the subject. What boy asked about babies?

"No. I'm fine being Uncle Angus. Maybe someday, an exceedingly long time from now, I'll find a woman for myself. I don't actively look." He shrugged.

"I don't look much either." She wanted to cringe when she saw Angus' lips twitch. She cooked the bacon and fried the eggs. "Pa, are you sure all you want is bread?"

"It's staying down. I don't want to eat anything else right now." The cabin was a small, one-room dwelling. Her pa was practically in the kitchen as he watched them from his bed.

Angus got the laudanum and mixed it with a bit of water.

"Here, Mr. Field," he said as he handed him a tin cup. "Would you like some help?"

"No, I think I can drink this without drownin' myself. You eat while the food is hot."

Angus sat and began eating. He took big bites and wiped his entire mouth when using the napkin. Much different from how she normally ate with her small amount of food on her fork and a dab at the corner of her mouth with the napkin. Maybe she could learn more than ranching from Angus. She needed to eat like a boy. Taking a deep breath, she dug in, spilling egg on her shirt. She used the whole napkin to wipe herself off. Her father's eyes were full of amusement. Ducking her head so she didn't laugh, she continued to eat.

"I'll do the bandaging if you clean up our mess," Angus offered.

"It's a deal." *Whew*, she was getting the better part of that one. She quickly cleaned up and was done by the time Angus finished. Then she put fresh water and more bread on a small table next to the bed.

"Pa, I will set the lamp here in case we get back after dark. Don't worry, it's just in case." She bent to kiss him, and he grunted. She froze. Right. No kissing, she'd have to ingrain what a boy would do instead of what she'd do. "See ya." She grabbed her too big hat and jammed it on her head.

It was bound to be an interesting day.

"Come on, put some muscle into it," Angus kidded. He thought he was teasing until Julian gave him a glare. He held up his hands in surrender. "I meant nothing by it. I'm just not used to feeding the animals in silence. There always seems to be some kind of ruckus going on at home with all my brothers."

"What's their names?" Julian made a show of using more of an exertion tossing hay into the stalls, and Angus suppressed a smile at the boy's efforts.

"There's Teagan, Quinn, Brogan, Sullivan, Donnell, Murphy, Fitzpatrick, Rafferty, and Shea."

Julian chuckled. "That is a bunch. I'm used to the quiet. When it's just me and Pa, we do some jawing, but not much."

A scuffling noise came from overhead followed by a soft yowl.

"What was that?" Angus cocked his head in the hayloft's direction.

"Just Claws, probably catching mice. She's good at it. She'll be a mama soon. I'd best go check on her." Julian scrambled up the ladder and called back down, "No mice, she's on her side, though. You reckon it's time?"

Angus climbed the ladder. There wasn't much standing room in the loft. "Where is Claws?"

"Down there near that pile of hay," Julian said, pointing.

Angus took a step closer and bumped into Julian. "Sorry—"

Julian pushed his way to the ladder and climbed down.

The boy was sure a puzzle. He looked mad. After his eyes adjusted to the dimmer light, Angus finally spotted a dark tabby cat nestled in some hay. "Claws is doing just fine," he called down. "We should check on her before supper, though." From his perch, he watched Julian leave the barn. Touchy and strange were good words for the boy.

Angus climbed down the ladder. Hopefully, there was a creek or something nearby to get a quick washing in later. He could barely stand the smell of himself in the hot weather. Julian could use a dousing too. Between them and Mr. Field, the air in the cabin would be beyond putrid. As he crossed the yard to the house, he noticed the two windows were open.

When was Rafferty going to stop by and bring him clean clothes? Maybe never, he conceded. Rafferty remembered nothing unless it had to do with the ranch. Everything else went in one ear and got lost. Angus took a breath of fresh air before he entered the cabin. Julian's pa was sitting in the small bed.

"Mr. Field, you're sitting up," he greeted the older man. "You're looking better already."

"Angus I wish I were. I'm sorry to have put you out."

"That's what neighbors are for. How many head do you think you run?" If the man answered five Angus wouldn't be surprised.

"Almost fifty. It's a bit much for the two of us, but I'm hoping to sell at least half and hire help."

"That's quite an accomplishment. That's a lot of cattle starting out. Where are they? I'm not insulting your land, but I see mostly rock."

"It was a tremendous disappointment when we got down here. I bought the land sight unseen. Fortunately, I had enough money for the land next to this ranch. But the only house and barn are on this side of the place. Big dreams I suppose, but we'll get there one step at a time. The good Lord is always looking out for us."

"You own all the land, including the Frederick ranch?" Angus had heard nothing about the Fredericks selling.

"Up to about an acre from their home. The oldest one, Sandy, said they were getting out of the cattle business," Jack Field explained.

Were their cattle still there? Sandy Frederick was on the shifty side. It wouldn't be beyond him to take advantage, but Angus sure hoped he hadn't. No sense getting anyone upset until he looked for himself.

Jack smiled when Julian handed him a plate of bread with a slice of ham. "Thank you."

"Angus, your meal is on the table," Julian said too politely. If that boy really planned to be a cowboy, he'd have to learn to say *"come and get the grub while it's hot"* or something like that, or no one would take him seriously.

"Good, I'm starved. Hard work does that, right Julian?"

Julian nodded and sat down almost... Angus frowned. "You and I will take a bath in the nice creek you have. Nothing like keeping clean. Don't you agree, Jack?"

"We're usually much cleaner," said Jack, breathing a bit hard with the effort of eating and speaking. "Poor Julian hasn't had time to wash clothes. Oh, and Julian, you might as well bathe in your union suit. It might be cold in the water."

Julian's eyes grew wide. "You know I can't wait to get bigger so I can be a cowboy like you, Angus, and like my pa. I keep waiting to grow taller and for muscles to get big, but nothing happens."

"Don't worry, Julian. We all grow in our own time. I think your voice will probably change first." Angus ate the food on his plate. He could have used more, but they seemed to have little. They'd get to hunting in a day or so, but in the meantime, he had another idea. "How about we go fishing tomorrow?"

Julian nodded and finished eating as Angus bowed his head.

Lord, this family needs Your help. Please heal Jack and please let the cattle still be there. I have a bad feeling, Lord, and if my thoughts are true help me stay calm. No one wants to see my temper. Help me give Julian confidence as a rancher. Thank You Lord.

"I'll clean up if you can grab soap and a couple o' towels for our dunking in the creek." Angus took all the plates to a small tub. He put the plates into it and added boiling water from the stove. He made sure he gathered everything that needed cleaning and dumped it all in. He'd noticed that Julian washed and then dried each item, immediately putting it away. Instead Angus washed the table and as he washed each dish, he set it on the table to dry. He carried the dirty water to the door and emptied it. When he turned back to the kitchen, Julian was drying the dishes and putting them away.

Angus sat next to Jack and put his hand on the other man's forehead. "Your fever is almost gone. How is the pain?"

"I'd like something to dull it." He shifted in the bed and winced. "Thank you for helping around the place. Julian has too much on… his shoulders. We have no other family. I know we just met, but if anything happens to me…" Jack closed his eyes.

"Don't worry, I have your back, Jack." Angus gently squeezed Jack's shoulder. He mixed the medicine with water and handed the glass to Jack. "We'll be back in a while."

SHE BREATHED SO FAST she thought she might pass out. This ruse had gone too far. She couldn't bathe with Angus. She'd taken her pa's hint and put on a cumbersome union suit and grabbed another clean one to change into. But it just wasn't right. What would Angus care if he found out? Why would it make a difference? He might leave, and they were coming to depend on his help. She grew glum when she pictured staying at home and not being allowed to ride the range. Part of her would wither if they curtailed her freedom.

Her ma had wanted to stay home cooking and cleaning, but there hadn't been much choice. They'd needed every hand to get the crop in. How her mother hated working outside, but she had always tried to put up a cheerful front.

Even when she grew weaker before she died, she insisted on helping.

Pa had loved her ma something fierce. He would touch her hand or kiss her cheek whenever they were near. Julian sighed. Maybe she'd have something like that someday. A knock on the door interrupted her musing.

Angus opened the door and smiled at the man on the other side. "Rafferty, I wasn't sure you'd bring my clean clothes. I thought maybe you'd lose them along the way." Angus grinned, obviously teasing.

"I was tempted to leave a trail of clothes, but just this once I thought I'd be nice."

"Come in, Rafferty, this is Jack Field and his son Julian." Rafferty gave her an odd look at first.

"Nice to meet you folks. I hope my brother has been minding his manners while he's been here." Rafferty laughed and offered a crooked grin. "I couldn't resist taunting Angus. He needs to loosen up a bit."

Despite the teasing, she could see the love they had for one another. It was lonely being an only child. They looked like brothers with their brown hair and blue eyes.

"Do you think you could bring an extra horse tomorrow?" Angus asked. "I want to go examine the cattle the Fredericks sold them."

Rafferty's eyes widened. "I'll bring the horse and help you find them." Rafferty's voice sounded grim.

"That would be a big help," Angus said.

"I'll see you tomorrow then. It was nice to meet you both." He didn't wait for replies, he was quickly out the door. Something wasn't right, she could feel it.

"I bought two fine geldings, but they were stolen a while back," Jack said.

"It's fine. We have more than enough horses. What did the sheriff say about the horses?"

"He said he'd look into it, but we never heard anything else. I can't thank you enough." Pa's eyes were shutting.

"Julian, we might as well go get cleaned up." Angus sounded as though he was looking forward to going down to the creek. All she wanted to do was drag her feet, but she couldn't think of an excuse not to clean herself.

They walked to the creek. The way there was much shorter than she remembered. What she'd give for storm clouds to roll in, but the sun shone brightly, making the water sparkle. Determined to keep her back to him, she walked up the creek a bit. Glancing over her shoulder, she paused until she was convinced he wasn't paying her any attention. She quickly stripped down to her overly big union suit. Her hands, feet and head were all that was unclothed. Still, it felt so very wrong.

As fast as she could, she got into the creek and hid her body under the cool water. But when she went to scrub herself, dismay filled her. *Oh no!* She'd left the soap with Angus. *This is ridiculous.* She started to scramble out. She hadn't realized Angus had closed the gap between them, and she gasped as his shadow fell across her.

"Here's the soap," he offered. He handed it to her with a nod and went back down to where he had been bathing.

Her limbs shook as she used the soap. It was all too much. Deceit was never good. It took a bit to get her breathing back under control. But Angus hadn't even noticed anything was amiss. She washed her hair and kept her back to him while she got out. Immediately she wrapped the towel around herself. She gathered her clean clothes and went behind the bushes nearby.

The entire ordeal must have taken years off her life. Daring she most certainly wasn't.

"Shy Julian?" Angus yelled to her. "Don't worry. I think every boy your age feels the same way."

She placed her hand over her heart. If she'd known that she wouldn't have panicked herself into exhaustion. She had to talk to Pa. He'd know what to do.

Carrying their belongings, they walked back to the house in silence. Everything was serene. Hopefully, she would have a chance to talk with Pa alone.

CHAPTER THREE

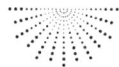

Something had Julian on edge. He certainly was a nervous boy. Tomorrow they'd check the cattle. Maybe getting out on the range would settle him some. Angus wanted to study the bill of sale, but it was doubtlessly so ambiguous it would be meaningless.

A scream startled him into running inside. There stood Julian by the bed with tears racing down his face. Jack lay lifeless, his eyes staring sightlessly. But for the first time since Angus had first walked in, Jack Field wore a look of peace on his face.

Without a word, Angus walked over and closed Jack's eyes. "I'm sorry, Julian. We did everything we could. He was comfortable when he passed." Angus shifted from foot to foot. He didn't know what else to say.

Julian placed his arms around him, and he stiffened, bewildered. He hugged the youngster and held him for a minute. Then he put the boy away from him. The lad needed to learn to stand on his own. It was a painful lesson for one so young. "I'll dig a grave. Any place in particular you'd prefer it?"

Mute, Julian shook his head.

Angus cringed at the sobs he heard once he was outside. It might take a miracle to toughen Julian up. He recalled spotting a shovel in the barn, and he stepped inside and grabbed it then continued to the nearest tree and began digging. The sound of the shovel hitting the dirt was all he could concentrate on. He was sweating by the time he finished, but he knew what he had to do. He'd take Julian to Dolly.

Julian couldn't bring herself to leave her pa's grave. She'd crushed the brim of her hat repeatedly, but her hands needed to be active. If only she could lie down next to his grave and weep, but she couldn't take the chance. She'd watched the expression in Angus' eyes; he thought her soft. He looked like he meant to make a man out of her. It wouldn't be the first time she'd seen such a look.

She snatched the shovel and looked for Claws. She was fine with two kittens next to her. Julian headed for the left corner of the house and dug until she heard the clang of metal striking metal. She sank to her knees and pushed dirt away until she easily lifted out the box. Hopefully, the papers meant she was now the owner of the land. Pa had so wished to make a good way of life for her. He'd been her rock her whole life.

Opening the box, she found the bill of sale for the ranch, the livestock, and the added land. She'd figure out a way. The Lord had invariably looked after her.

"Are those the documents for this place?"

She turned and nodded, handing them to him. "I can continue on. It's all mine."

Angus nodded and carried the papers inside, reading as

he walked. His head shook ominously, and her heart plummeted. Something was awry. She needed to ask, but she'd had enough upset for one day. Finally, after a few deep breaths, she screwed up the courage.

"Angus, what's the matter?" She grimaced when he shifted his gaze to her. The pounding in her chest was all she could hear.

"Let's sit." Angus turned a chair and straddled it. He set the papers on the table.

She sat at the table and waited for him to start.

"I don't know how to tell you this and it's not fair after the day you've had, but it's always best to recognize the truth." He hesitated and drew in a heavy breath. "These documents mean nothing. The Fredericks are crooks. Look at this wording." Angus pointed out the words on the paper. *The property. The cattle. The horses.* "It doesn't identify what property or livestock this document is about. I wish someone could have warned you."

Clasping her shaking fists, she placed them on top of the table. "What about the ranch? Do I own the ranch?"

"That depends on how old you are."

Glancing at her hands, she shrugged her right shoulder. What was the correct answer? "I'm… nineteen."

He groaned as he rubbed his face with his hand. "I know you're not that old. You need not shave and you're too small to be nineteen. Tell you what, pack a bag and we'll go to my ranch for a few days while I get this all straightened out. I can claim the ranch, but for the rest." He shook his head. "I doubt the law will allow you to own any of it."

She peered at him through damp lashes. What had happened to the world? How could someone cheat her and her pa that way? She bit the inside of her cheek to keep from crying. "I'll pack," she said, feeling utterly disheartened.

There wasn't much to gather. It never mattered to her.

Material possessions were insignificant. Finally, she stared at the bed her father had died in. It hurt to draw a breath. She pulled all the bedding off and set it outside. Then she cleaned the dishes before she finally threw out food that would spoil.

"I'm ready to leave. I need to get Claws and her kittens. The papers…"

Angus patted his chest. "I have the papers right here in my pocket. The kittens are so tiny. I don't think we should move them just yet."

"How come she only had two?"

"I don't know Julian. Don't worry I'll come and collect them in a few days.

She took one last glance around the cabin before she followed him and lightly closed the door.

CHAPTER FOUR

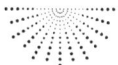

*I*t'd been rough to watch Julian trying not to cry. He was being as brave as he could. Angus reined Julian's bay in at the ranch house, grateful the old horse had had it in him to carry them back to the Kavanagh spread. Sheila, Sullivan, and Dolly all hurried outside.

Sullivan lifted his brow, and Angus shook his head.

"I'm so sorry, Julian," Sheila said.

"Me too, I'm Sullivan." Sullivan held out his hand to Julian after he'd jumped to the ground.

"Thank you," Julian replied.

Dolly drew a solid look at the boy before she bustled over and embraced him. "You poor, poor boy." She nodded to Angus. "You were wise to bring him here."

Angus gave Dolly a quick smile. "Take care of him while I put up the horse?" He didn't need to wait for a confirmation. He knew Julian would be in the finest of hands with Dolly.

The Kavanagh brothers had lost their mother when they were young, and then their father had died as well. Dolly had been the only parent in their lives. She was the family's constant, with unconditional love they could count on.

Angus put the old horse into a stall and then brushed him down. Poor old thing looked like it might drop any day. On his way out of the barn, he stopped by Captain's stall. "Looks like we need to pick out a horse for Julian. Any suggestions?" His horse nuzzled him, looking for a treat. Angus chuckled. "Fine, think about it, though."

What was he going to do with Julian? From recent history, whoever brought a lost soul to the ranch ended up being responsible for that person. There would be no problem showing him how to work the ranch, but what was he supposed to do with the lad when they weren't working?

"Need a hand?" Sullivan asked.

"I'm about done here. It's been an interminable day."

Sullivan nodded and then took off his hat. He ran his fingers through his hair. "What are you going to do about that rock patch of a ranch?"

"I'll buy it. Julian's father is buried there. I'll set aside the money for the boy's future. I'd like to make the Fredericks' pay. The boy's people were sharecroppers. Can you imagine how often they had to go without trying to save enough to buy a ranch, let alone livestock and additional land?"

Sullivan gazed at him. "I'm shocked you haven't gone to the Fredericks' yet."

Angus grinned. "What do you mean? I never go half-cocked. I'm trying to take hold of my temper. I noted at the last barn dance many of the ladies avoided me."

"I think it's more that you speak your mind and less your temper. Telling a young woman her dress doesn't look good on her is no way to make friends."

"Either way, I doubt the Fredericks are going anywhere. Plus, I need to help get Julian settled. I hope no one thinks I overstepped with bringing him here."

Sullivan snorted. "Since when did you care what we

thought? I think it's a fine thing you brought the young-un here. I bet Dolly has him eating by now."

"We can all have a hand in helping him." Angus carefully planted the seed of Julian being everybody's concern.

"Oh no, brother. He's your responsibility, but I don't mind showing him how to run a ranch seeing as I'm the finest at it." Sullivan grinned. "We might as well go to the ranch house before you list off the reasons, you're best at it."

"You're right, the list is considerably lengthy." Angus smiled. There was nothing better than having brothers.

JULIAN MINDED her manners while interacting with Dolly and Sheila. Her pa had repeatedly told her to read the individuals surrounding her and to act accordingly. When with a bunch of cowboys act rough around the edges, but with women be polite. It was hard enough trying to be a boy.

Dolly kept studying her. Had Dolly somehow discerned her secret? The chance of discovery was the reason she had always kept to herself. When it would be safe to *be* herself, her pa had never said. It still was the best option that folks thought her a boy. Her heart hurt. He'd never tell her when it was safe now. She was an orphan.

"How old are you, Julian?" Dolly asked as she set a piece of apple pie on the table.

Julian swallowed hard and took a gulp of milk, reminding herself that nineteen didn't fly with Angus. "I'm sixteen, ma'am."

"Call me Dolly. We're casual around here. Do you have other relatives you'd like us to contact for you?"

Was Dolly looking for a way to be rid of her? "No, it was just me and Pa. I realize he's with the Lord now. He was an honorable man. I'm only glad he died thinking he had a fine herd. He wished to be sure he set my future and I wouldn't be wanting. I can move back to my ranch, ma'am. I know you have a whole lot of people here, and you need not take on one more. I'm perfectly capable of handling things." She pretended the pie fascinated her as she ate it, afraid if she looked up Dolly would doubtless give her a sympathetic *you have to leave* look.

"We have plenty of room for you. In fact, you'll have a room of your own."

"I'm— That is, I could sleep in the barn. This house is too fine for the likes of me. I've been nowhere so nice." Julian glanced at Dolly and then at Sheila. They were both complicated to read. If they knew she wasn't a boy, they sure weren't saying anything.

Dolly's eye brightened when Angus and Sullivan stepped inside. "I think you and Angus can work it all out. He'll be your guardian."

Julian widened her eyes and turned her head to meet Angus' bewildered gaze. "I don't require a guardian." She relaxed when Angus nodded.

"Don't be silly. Gemma and her children will be down shortly. So, you like children?"

"Ma'am—Dolly, I don't know. I haven't been around many. All I know is they are one more mouth to feed." By the surprise in Dolly's eyes, she knew she'd stepped in it. But she'd heard people complain about another mouth to feed for as long as she could remember.

Angus took a step toward Julian. "Speaking of mouths… never mind. Let's get you set up in the empty bedroom. Is that fine with you, Dolly?"

"Perfect."

"Come on, Julian, I'll show you around the house."

Angus walked down a hall quickly and she had to scurry to catch up to him. He opened a door and she followed him into a bedroom. She'd never slept in her own room before. "This is awfully big. I don't belong here."

Angus sat on the bed. "You'll get used to it. Don't worry about the guardian thing. At the same time, don't go getting into any trouble with the law. I'd have to be the one to go get you out of jail." Angus chuckled.

A slight smile was all she could summon. "I don't plan on that happening." Having a guardian wasn't sitting well with her. How much did she even know about Angus?

"Come on, boy, I'll show you around."

CHAPTER FIVE

Three days later
"Angus, come out back, we need to talk to you," Dolly said as she stood next to Gemma.

He grimaced but held the door wide for the women. They strolled a distance from the house. Must be a secret or something.

Gemma cleared her throat. "I'm not suggesting this because I'm Teagan's wife or because I'm trying to tell you what to do. I like Julian, really I do—"

"He is required to bathe and put on clean clothes," Dolly finished.

Angus opened his mouth and then promptly shut it.

"He's always so helpful, but Angus, he stinks," Dolly continued. "I'm afraid one of the older children will mention something and the poor lad has no confidence as it is. I don't know if you noted, but he looks to you before he undertakes anything. You've been good with him, teaching him, and I've heard you tell him he's doing a great job. I have no complaint about anything except for Julian's hygiene habits."

Gemma nodded. "Take him to the pond or the stream. Make sure he can swim, well actually forget the stream. Brenna almost drowned in it. Use the pond or the tub but scrub him down. I venture once he grow's whiskers and has to shave he'll learn to wash up, but I suspect he's younger than he told Dolly."

Angus nodded. "I know he's not nineteen."

"He told me sixteen," Dolly said, amused. "I'm thinking twelve, maybe thirteen. More because of looks, but he's a very mature boy. I bet he had to grow up fast. Did you arrange the deed for the land?"

"I did and it's in my name, but we're all aware the ranch is Julian's. I visited a lawyer, and I was correct about the land and livestock documents. They are meaningless, and the sheriff claimed he doesn't have enough proof to arrest the Fredericks. We need to keep an eye on them. They're running out of folks to swindle. They'll probably move on to rustling next. Julian is in the barn. I'll grab clean clothes and towels for the both of us and take him to the pond."

"Soap, take loads of soap," Gemma insisted.

"I appreciate your help in the matter." A smile spread across his face. It was a relief that they didn't have something more important to discuss. Women! Even though, in this case, they were right. He could still hear them talking when he reached the backdoor.

He was right, Julian was in the barn mucking out stalls. "Hey, we need to make ourselves nice and clean."

Julian shook his head. "We already bathed this month."

"We have no choice if we wish to step foot in the house. I should have taken you with me the other day."

Angus glanced at his oldest brother Teagan and they shared a moment of agreement without having to talk.

"You two run on. Just don't take all day about it," Teagan said. His lips twitched as though he would laugh.

Julian practically dragged his feet the whole path to the pond. Angus didn't know what to say to the sullen child.

"It's a good size pond. Not deep, though. It's convenient for washing, fishing, and watering the cattle. We have a rule because it is obscured from view when you wander from the house you need to call out. This way if any of the ladies are bathing you don't end up seeing something you shouldn't." He angled his head and stared hard at the boy. "You follow what I mean, don't you?"

"I understand, but most individuals prefer privacy, not just the women. I don't take my clothes off in front of anyone, never." His face grew to a dark shade of crimson.

Angus stared at Julian. How had he managed to have privacy in a one-room cabin?

"Well, I'll keep my back turned if you do the same. How's that?"

Julian hesitated before he nodded. "Sounds fair enough, but I'm leaving my union suit on."

"I've never known you to be stubborn before," Angus observed. "I will have to say a big no. That union suit probably stinks. It won't help in your goal to get washed. Now, if we stop jawing about it, we can get it done right quick." Angus tossed clothes, a towel, and a sliver of soap to Julian.

Angus did as promised; he kept his back turned even in the nice cool water. He heard washing and that's all he needed. Julian was a shy one. Maybe because he didn't have any brothers. It was strange for sure, but it would work itself out.

"Go on and get out. I'll place my back to you. Give me a shout when you're dressed." Angus waited; the boy didn't dawdle. Julian probably was younger than he'd guessed, and maybe he was trying to hide it.

"I'm done! I'm going to race back while you get dressed. Thanks, Angus!"

Chuckling, Angus threw back his head and looked up at the heavens.

Lord, I will need Your help. Help me be patient and help me be the man a boy would be proud to have as his guardian. Guide me in teaching Julian right from wrong. I don't know why You picked me to be there for Julian, but I will do right by him with Your help.

He plucked up the towel left behind by the young-un. He was an agreeable fellow, and he tried so hard. Sometimes he just didn't have the strength to get some jobs completed, but that would come with age and some growing. Whistling, he stepped back home.

JULIAN COULDN'T STOP SHIVERING, and it had nothing to do with being cold. That had been a close call. Was it worth pretending to be a boy? Would it matter to the Kavanaghs in the long run? Lying was wrong, but it was self-preservation. Her pa had considered it the only course, and she'd go along with it until it wasn't possible.

Luckily, she had a slight build. When she viewed herself in the mirror, she never saw the hint of curves like other females. What would it be like to have long hair? Gemma had beautiful coffee brown hair. It was thick, and she brushed it one hundred times every night Julian had heard her say to Dolly. She had long eyelashes and she exuded kindness with her smiles.

Most women were married by the age of nineteen. Still, she was grateful she was safe and Angus protected her. He was comfortable to be around most of the time. He'd probably despise her when he knew the truth. He wasn't one to fool with.

"Well, don't you look handsome!" Dolly gave her a quick embrace. "We go to church tomorrow. Do you trust in God?"

"Yes, Ma'am my parents raised me to be a good Christian. It's not always straightforward, but I try. I haven't been to church since we bought the homestead. I'll look forward to it." She hesitated. "I don't have proper church clothes." Julian stared at her feet. She didn't need to see the look of pity Dolly most likely wore. Who wouldn't feel sorry for her? Her pa raised her to hold her head high, but it wasn't so simple.

"I'll find something for you to wear. In fact, I expect we have plenty of boy's clothes in the attic. I saved them all. You can look tomorrow afternoon if you like."

She lifted her head and smiled at Dolly. "Thank you. I don't want folks to pity me. There is no shame in living a moral, decent life especially if you are hardworking and have the best interest of others in your heart. But I loathe the stares I occasionally get."

"You'll go far in life, Julian. You have a wonderful outlook on life, especially for someone so young. You might teach Angus a thing or two."

Angus rounded the corner of the house. "Did I hear my name?"

Dolly nodded. "More than likely. You're just in time for supper."

"Julian I brought you a surprise."

Julian raced to Angus "I bet it's Claws, Paws and Jaws! Where are they?"

"In the second stall in the nearest barn."

Julian hardly waited for Angus to finish talking. She ran to the barn and opened the stall door. "Oh, Claws look at you and your babies. Why they look almost like you, but the stripes are a bit different. I'm so glad you are here." She picked up the nearest kitten. "Welcome Paws." She snuggled the kitten. Leaning over she touched the other kitten. "Glad to see you Jaws."

"Jaws?"

She glanced up and there stood Angus.

"I came up with Paws and I wanted the other name to rhyme. Jaws rhymes."

Angus chuckled. "Indeed it does."

CHAPTER SIX

*J*ulian ran her palms over the shirt Dolly had given her. She'd worn nothing so soft. The sleeves had to be turned up, but she didn't mind. The trousers fit just right. She combed her hair back and then surveyed herself in the mirror. She appeared to be a young boy. The wives on the ranch weren't much older than she, but they looked feminine. It was helpful that she looked like a boy, but it didn't feel great. Was she wrong to yearn for a smile from an admirer? Yes, she decided, she probably was. Sighing, she turned from the mirror and fled outside.

"Wagon or horseback?" Angus asked.

"Horseback of course," she responded. She dashed to the barn. Angus had promised to choose a horse for her to use as hers. They'd turned her old bay out to pasture.

Angus caught up. "This gray is named Smokey. I expect the two of you will get along just fine."

Her eyes grew wide. She'd never ridden a horse so tall. Too bad there wasn't a smaller horse, one that looked more like a pony than a giant. "Th-thank you, Angus. I will need help to saddle him. I can't reach that high."

Angus chuckled. "You'll be sprouting like a weed soon enough, Julian. I don't mind helping for a time."

They worked together getting Captain and Smokey saddled and bridled. Angus lifted her by the waist and plunked her into the saddle. He wasn't gentle, but then, he wouldn't feel the need to be with a boy.

Once up there, her stomach plunged. It was a long way down, but she was determined to show Angus she could accomplish anything a cowboy could. Angus mounted up in one smooth move. He'd hate to realize she considered him limber. She smiled.

"Ready?" Angus asked. He looked particularly nice in his Sunday church clothes.

She nodded and kneed Smokey. He had a nice smooth gait and plenty of energy. It took a lot of strength to keep him moving at a slower pace. They'd get on just fine. Perfect as soon as she reached her *growth spurt*. Another smile curved her lips. Angus meant well.

The church was lovely with a flower garden the likes she'd never seen. A tear appeared in her eye when she spotted the cemetery. *I miss you, Pa.*

Wagons full of Kavanaghs pulled up, and she found herself amid a great deal of noise until everyone was inside and settled. She perched at the end of a pew with Angus beside her. Through most of the service she had plenty of room, but one child refused to sit in either Quinn or Heaven's lap, so everyone shifted to make room for the little one. Julian found herself smooshed between the wooden edge and Angus.

His shoulders were bigger and harder than she'd guessed. He took up a lot of room. His elbow struck her ribs, causing her to bite her lip, so she didn't cry out. Turning her head, she peered around for an empty seat, but all she saw were creepy smiles from little girls. What age did girls around here seek to gain the regard of the boys?

She sat as still as possible and listened to the preacher. He was droning on and on about money needed for a park for children to play. What did that even mean? The whole outdoors was a park created by God. Money should go to the poor and unfortunate. But… he was the preacher, so he must be right.

When her family would attend services, they had remained in the back with the other poor folk. She had never given it much thought before, but wasn't that unfair? Weren't people all God's children? Now the preacher was reading from the Bible. This part she liked. Sharing a Bible with Angus was a bit much, but she wanted to hear and read the words of God.

Book of John, Chapter 4

Beloved, believe not every spirit, but try the spirits whether they are of God: because many false prophets are gone out into the world.

Hereby know *ye the Spirit of God: Every spirit that confesseth that Jesus Christ is come in the flesh is of God:*

And every spirit *that confesseth not that Jesus Christ is come in the flesh is not of God: and this is that spirit of antichrist, whereof ye have heard that it should come; and even now already is it in the world.*

Ye are of God, *little children, and have overcome them: because greater is he that is in you, than he that is in the world.*

. . .

THEY ARE OF THE WORLD: therefore speak they of the world, and the world heareth them.

WE ARE OF GOD: he that knoweth God heareth us; he that is not of God heareth not us. Hereby know we the spirit of truth, and the spirit of error.

BELOVED, let us love one another: for love is of God; and every one that loveth is born of God, and knoweth God.

HE THAT LOVETH not knoweth not God; for God is love.

IN THIS WAS MANIFESTED the love of God toward us, because that God sent his only begotten Son into the world, that we might live through him.

HEREIN IS LOVE, not that we loved God, but that he loved us, and addressed his Son to be the propitiation for our sins.

BELOVED, if God so loved us, we ought also to love one another.

NO MAN HATH seen God at any time. If we love one another, God dwelleth in us, and his love is perfected in us.

HEREBY KNOW we that we dwell in him, and he in us, because he hath given us of his Spirit.

. . .

And we have seen and do testify that the Father sent the Son to be the Saviour of the world.

Whosoever shall confess that Jesus is the Son of God, God dwelleth in him, and he in God.

And we have known and believed the love that God hath to us. God is love; and he that dwelleth in love dwelleth in God, and God in him.

Herein is our love made perfect, that we may have boldness in the day of judgment: because as he is, so are we in this world.

There is no fear in love; but perfect love casteth out fear: because fear hath torment. He that feareth is not made perfect in love.

We love him, because he first loved us.

If a man say, I love God, and hateth his brother, he is a liar: for he that loveth not his brother whom he hath seen, how can he love God whom he hath not seen?

And this commandment have we from him, That he who loveth God love his brother also.

. . .

Warmth swept through Julian as all appeared brighter. Peace filled her along with a renewal of her love for God. A happiness she'd never experienced before came over her. She would be fine. Her faith was steadfast and forever flourishing. Fear that had weighed her down lifted from her shoulders.

"Are you all right?" Angus whispered.

"Yes, everything is more than fine."

CHAPTER SEVEN

*T*here was something peculiar about Julian. Angus sat at his favorite fishing spot, waiting to catch a fish while casting frequent glances at Julian. He looked as though all his doubts were gone. Fishing could be calming, but this seemed like something more.

"What are you pondering about?" Angus asked.

"God. I feel closer to Him."

"That's always a positive thing. It was a narrow fit in the pew. You need to eat more. I noticed just how skinny you are. You're doing the work of a man, you need to eat like one."

Julian started to nod but ended up shaking his head. "Maybe when I hit my growth spurt."

"Could be. Was your family religious?" How did one feel closer to God?

"The only book we ever owned was the Bible. We read it a lot, and the words of God sustained us in the hard times. Yes, I suppose my family was religious. I never gave it much attention. I assumed everyone praised the Lord and lived by His teachings."

Angus smiled. "Sounds to me you have spent limited time around individuals who don't believe in God."

Julian shrugged. "I think you're correct. Do you think telling a nontruth in the name of keeping yourself safe is the devil's work?"

The boy sure did talk strangely sometimes. *A non-what?* "Oh, you mean lying? That's between the liar and God. God probably would prefer the person to be protected, but honestly, what do I know?" Angus narrowed his eyes. "Is someone lying to you?"

"I don't think so." Julian's pole dipped toward the water. "There's a fish on my hook! It's heavy, I need your help!" His voice screeched, and he quickly peeked at Angus.

"Don't be embarrassed. Your voice is just changing." He grabbed the pole from the boy and lifted the fish from the water. "This is huge! But we'll need more if we want to feed the entire family."

BUT JULIAN DIDN'T CARE about the size of the fish. "My voice is changing? How long before it should be totally changed?" Her heart pounded.

Angus shrugged. "It depends."

Fisting her hands, she tried to appear calm. "On what?" He was taking his time answering and she wanted to shake him.

"Teagan's voice seemed to change all at once while mine changed gradually. I had many embarrassing squeaking moments. The fact is, no one else seems to notice much. Not as much as you notice your own voice."

Breathing deeply, she relaxed her hands. "We'd best get fishing if we're gonna catch more." She took her pole and baited her hook before she sat back down.

"You seem upset." Angus studied her. "It happens to us all. Didn't your pa tell you what to expect as you grew?" He threw his line back in the water.

A web of lies. She was creating a web of lies. One lie continued into another, and again another. Her Pa had declared she'd be a boy until they built the ranch and they could afford to hire help. That wasn't her future anymore. Her stomach clenched painfully.

"You'll probably see a whisker or two starting to grow on your chin," Angus explained. "How old are you again?"

"How old did I tell you?" Here it was. They'd finally caught her. She could sense the intensity of his gaze, but she couldn't bear to glance at him. He was bound to show his disappointment, and his opinion meant too much.

"I don't want to know what you *told* me," pressed Angus. "How old *are* you?"

"I…well, I don't exactly know." She peered at him through her eyelashes.

His frown deepened. He apparently didn't believe her. "Julian, we all have our shortcomings. I can forgive just about anything but not lies. I need to be able to trust the people in my life. If I were in trouble, I need to be able to trust you'll do the right thing whether it's running and getting help or hiding; whatever I tell you needs doing. You understand?"

She nodded slowly and then closed her eyes. A lone tear slipped out and the wetness trailed down her face. What was she going to do? Being alone like this would be considered unseemly. Learning to be a cowboy would end. Building her own ranch would never come true.

She opened her eyes and made certain she didn't glance Angus' way. Standing up, she lay down her stick and walked away. She heard him call to her, but she kept her head down and continued walking.

When she walked through the house to her room, she

could feel eyes upon her. Shame engulfed her as she closed the door and lay on her bed. It might not be her room for long. She needed to find out about the ranch. What age did she have to be to inherit—if she could inherit at all? Could a woman own property?

Lord forgive me, please. It probably isn't appropriate to ask forgiveness for something I continue to do. Angus must hate me, and he's my dearest friend. I realize I have to go through the hard times to get to the good. My pa said he had two happy days; when he married my ma and when I was born. I expect he was also happy when he bought the ranch. We had plenty of lean times, but he never complained. Do I only get a limited number of happy days? Have I used them and not realized it? Lord, will all my days be a trial from now on? I'm ashamed I've been lying to these honest people. I don't know what to do, or what will happen? I'm not brave enough. Please make me brave, Lord. Amen.

For the first time, praying didn't lighten her troubles. It made her feel worse. She was deliberately walking down the wrong path. Tossing and turning on the bed, she realized what she had to do.

CHAPTER EIGHT

Julian rummaged through her sack and eventually found what she'd been searching for. A wrinkled dress of her mother's. It had been wrinkled since her mother's death; there had been no reason to iron it.

Holding it up against her, she glanced in the mirror. She made a better-looking cowboy than she did a woman. Bravery was within her somewhere; she just needed to locate it. She didn't have all the undergarments, but it wouldn't matter much. They'd probably order her to leave first thing anyway.

She undressed and slipped on the worn and wrinkled brown dress. The fit wasn't bad, even though it was loose. Taking a deep breath, she opened the door to join the others for supper. God was with her; she could do this.

It seemed like the longest walk ever as she plodded down the hall. The family could all be heard. She'd best go in there before one of the children spotted her and gave her away. Hesitantly she entered the vast room and little by little it got quieter until there was silence.

"I have something to tell you all."

"You're a *woman?*" Angus' eyes blazed with fury. "I told you I couldn't tolerate lies!" He gave her a lengthy look before he stomped out of the house.

Her stomach churned, and she grew afraid she'd be sick. Staring at her feet, she continued. "My pa thought it for the best that I disguise myself as a boy. I've worn boy clothes for ten years, ever since my ma died. We lived in a place where some men just helped themselves to the girls and threw them aside after. Pa didn't want that for me. I should have told you, but I didn't know how." Tears rolled down her face. "I know lying is a sin and I'm asking for your forgiveness."

Arms came around her and she knew it was Dolly. "Of course. Your father only wanted you protected. We've lived in such unsettled times. I'm glad you told us."

Once the tears stopped flowing, Julian stepped back and gave Dolly a small smile. "Thank you. I upset Angus."

Brenna and Fitzpatrick came to her side and helped her to the table. "Sit, Julian, I'll pour you some tea," Brenna said.

Julian didn't miss the expression of surprise the couple shared. Did they assume the worst of her? Glancing around, she saw sympathy. Someone needed to be outraged for Angus' sake. Was no one going after him?

"But Angus—"

"Is a grown man and needs to sort things out for himself," Teagan told her. "It'll be fine, you'll see."

Would she see? What if Angus hated her permanently? Her heart shattered. At least she would not continue to lie. That must count for something. Or maybe not as far as Angus was concerned. She yearned to run after him, but that wasn't sensible.

"Thank you," she said to Brenna as a cup of tea was placed in front of her. Brenna and Fitzpatrick hadn't been married long ,and their happiness was there for all to observe.

"Julian, after supper I'd like to speak to you," Dolly said. Julian nodded as her stomach clenched harder.

"Yes, ma'am."

Throughout supper she felt them staring at her as she kept her gaze on her plate and slowly ate. It was a relief they didn't ask questions. Waiting to talk to Dolly was daunting. Would she be asked to leave? She'd be fine, she'd have a roof over her head.

Time went slowly when a body was dreading something.

"Julian, let's go out back."

Julian stood and followed Dolly outside. She took as many deep breaths as she could, struggling to calm herself.

"Dolly, I'm so sorrowful. There isn't an excuse for my lies."

"Sweetheart, sit." She gestured to a chair. Dolly seated herself in the chair opposite.

"I'm not here to lecture you. I'm concerned is all. If you don't want to answer any question tell me so. It's fine. Have you been married before?"

"No."

"What about other family?"

"I have no one."

"How old are you?"

"I'm nineteen. Old enough to know better." Julian glanced elsewhere.

"Did any man try to take you?"

"No, not that I know of. My pa was very protective. He didn't care if the ranch we purchased was a bunch of big rocks, he wanted to start someplace new. I think he meant for me to shed my boy clothes soon enough and get married. He talked about grandchildren."

"One last question. How close have you and Angus become?"

Julian opened her eyes wide. Surprise went through her.

"What do you mean? He looked out for me and was teaching me how to be a cowboy."

"I don't expect he had an inkling. We all just figured you were an awkward fellow," Dolly explained. She gazed out across the land and sighed.

"I don't know what Texas law is. I don't know if women may own property or what age I have to be to not have a guardian. I feel stupid. I never needed to know any of that before Pa died."

Dolly leaned over and patted her hand. "I'm sure Angus will figure it all out for you. He just requires time. Meanwhile, you can help me here at the house."

Her heart sank; no more learning how to ranch. "Thank you, I'd be happy to help."

"THINGS COULD BE WORSE," Rafferty told Angus as they watched the horses frolicking in the grass.

Angus frowned. "How could it be worse? How exactly could it be worse?"

"I'll come up with something. Give me a few minutes." Rafferty chuckled. His merriment stopped when Angus glared at him.

"What am I supposed to do now? I'm guardian to a girl—no make that a woman. A boy would have been easy. I could provide clothes and food, a place to sleep and ranching knowhow. Am I supposed to go into town and buy clothes for her? For a grown woman? I'd never live it down. This whole matter is making me queasy." He ran his palm over his face. "We bathed in the pond together!" His heart pounded painfully against his ribs. They'd slept in the same bed together though only the two of them knew *that*. "Do you think she was seeking to trap me as her husband? This is an outrage!"

Rafferty shook his head. "Don't let this bring your temper back. She isn't cunning enough to have tried to hoodwink you into marriage. Besides, there are other options. She didn't have to choose the Kavanagh with the biggest nose. You work all the time; you have no time for a wife."

Angus' face heated. He whirled around and pushed Rafferty's shoulder hard enough to make him stumble back. "You can't have her unless I approve of it, you rotten—"

"Stop!" Julian stood near them with her eyes wide and her hand over her mouth. Her expression was one of fear. Tears filled her eyes as she wrapped her arms around her waist.

"I think I hear someone calling me!" Rafferty hurried to the house.

Closing his eyes, Angus turned his back on her. He'd started to love the boy like a brother, but now, he'd have to find a place to send her. Surely there were places for young ladies he could afford.

"Angus?" Her voice was scarcely a whisper.

What if he pretended, he didn't hear her? Maybe he could just walk away. It wasn't his pride that stung the most, his emotions were all in a chaotic jumble with anger at the top.

He turned and found that her eyes were wet and red. The frock she wore was the ugliest he'd ever seen. Her hair would be deemed a woman's nightmare. He'd been made a fool of, and that didn't set well with him. He glared at her.

"Is your name really Julian or did you make that up too?"

"I was named after my mother's father. Julian is my name," she said softly. She reached down and picked up Claws.

"Did you enjoy our conversation about growing into a man? I'm uncertain what you are after with your little charade, but I'm beyond livid. It would be in your best benefit to go back to the house. Now!"

She jumped and gave him a long stare before she put down the cat and ran to the house.

It was as though he'd lost a friend. He'd looked forward to teaching Julian about ranching and helping him develop into a man of integrity. The boy had essentially died, and Angus was mourning him.

CHAPTER NINE

Julian scurried out of the way anytime Angus was near. He acted as though he couldn't bear to be in the same room as her. His loathing for her was so strong she felt it constantly. His glares shriveled her heart, but she couldn't fault him. His disdain had been earned.

It had been three days and his feelings were clear to everyone. The tension in the house was immeasurable. God had answered her prayers; she'd been nothing but brave. It would have been easier to remain in her room. Every morning she gathered her courage and with a straight back walked into the kitchen.

The complete family knew she was a liar. Her name was muddied, and that hurt. She'd tried so hard to be perfect the last few days, it exhausted her. She asked for nothing, and she followed Dolly's instruction. Now and again she'd stare out the window and realize her yearning was to be ranching.

Smokey probably wasn't her horse anymore. Besides being big, he wasn't a proper slow horse for a female.

"Teagan, can I talk to you in your office?" she inquired

while gazing at the floor. She carried too much shame to look anyone in the eye.

"Come, I have time now." His voice was so tender it made her want to sob. He closed the door and gestured for her to sit.

"First, I'm so sorry about my betrayal of your trust. I'd been pretending to be a boy for as long as I can remember. My pa said it was safer. I realize it's no excuse." She sighed. "I need to know about the legalities of my ranch ownership and the guardianship." The lump in her throat grew greater with each word.

"Angus owns the ranch."

She gasped.

"As far as guardianship, I know he had papers drawn up. He wanted to be sure you weren't taken and placed in a boys' home. The age of consent in Texas is ten years old, but with legal papers I'm not sure."

"I'm homeless." The sobs she'd been holding in escaped her. She bent and buried her head in her lap. She heard Teagan leave and she sobbed harder. What was to become of her? *Oh Pa, what should I do?*

Things wouldn't have been so bad if she still owned the ranch. She stood when the door burst open and Angus stepped in. With a nod, he shut the door.

"I was told to come in here and explain matters to you." He paced behind the desk and managed to not glance at her. "The guardianship is until you are twenty, and yes I own the ranch. You will stay here until you are twenty, at which point we can decide your future." Without another word or giving her the opportunity to ask questions, he abruptly strode out of the room.

Twenty? She had ten more months to go. She wanted the ranch back; her father lay at rest there. Perhaps in ten months she could get it? Angus had been harsher than harsh.

Her legs shook as she stood, and she held on to the back of the chair until she steadied herself.

There was laundry to do. Women's work. Not ranch work.

She could see most of the brothers' houses from where she scrubbed the clothing. They had all waved to her. She watched as they tended a communal garden and ran after their children. Brenna was busy with wash of her own. It was good to stay busy.

She needed to plan for her future. There had to be a means for her to make a bit of money. Not for things, but for her day of freedom. She'd never created a dress before, but Dolly had shown her where a bit of cloth was.

She plucked up a shirt to rub against the scrub board and her heart squeezed as she recognized the blue checked material. It belonged to Angus. Thankfully, it didn't smell like him anymore. He had a unique essence of leather and a deep woody smell. She'd never be close enough to him to catch his scent again.

Thoughts such as these needed to stop and stop now. There were realities, the biggest being she no longer owned her ranch. Learning that had shaken her to the core. Her pa had bought the land, so she'd always have a home.

She'd never felt so alone before. Even Claws was busy with her own family. The whinny of a horse caught her attention. She abandoned the garden and went to the corral. She'd never seen a horse so light in color before. He was so beautiful, like he'd been made of gold.

"A palomino, he's quite the handful."

Julian turned to the right and nodded to the lanky blond man. "I've never seen a horse like it before."

"I'm Donald Dill. I work with the horses."

She smiled. "I'm Julian. I'm… new here. Do you break the horses?"

He grinned and his blue eyes twinkled. "How do you like Smokey?"

"Smokey isn't mine anymore. He's too tall for a female anyway, I guess." Her face warmed as she kept her eyes lowered.

"Maybe. Did you like his gait?"

She met his gaze and nodded. "He possesses a very smooth gait. He's a powerful horse and he's gentle. I would have been thrilled with him. I'm sure Angus will pick out an older, docile horse for me to ride."

"We have a few of those too. I'll ask Angus about it. Are you planning to stay around?"

"I don't expect I have a choice. Angus is in charge of my fate. That is for the next ten months. You've probably heard the story."

He gave her a caring smile. "Yes, ma'am, I have."

"Call me Julian if you like." She admired his deep, vibrant voice. "Is this horse ready to ride?"

Donald stared at the horse and grinned. "He and I are having a difference of opinion about that at the moment. I'll try again tomorrow."

"Why wait until tomorrow?"

Donald chuckled. "That's the way some people break horses but I like a slower, gentler method. I think everyone has their own technique. Some horses are harder to train than others. This one thinks he's outsmarted me, and he thinks he's won. He'll be put out tomorrow when we do the same thing. He'll be an amazing horse when I'm finished."

She wished she could think of something to add. Her mind was vacant.

"You're welcome to come by anytime and watch. I will ask Angus about Smokey. Are you two betrothed?"

Julian chuckled, but then a sense of melancholy came over her. "No. He became stuck being my guardian. I will stay out of his way as much as I can."

He tilted his head as he studied her face. "That's got to be hard. If you need anything or a shoulder to cry on, I'm always here. Why don't I get you after supper and I can introduce you to the horses?"

Her breath caught. This man was offering friendship, and she intended to grasp it. "I'll be delighted. I have more work to complete. It's been nice to meet you Donald."

"Likewise." He grinned.

CHAPTER TEN

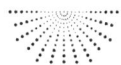

*A*ngus didn't join them for supper. He was dining with the other cowboys. Julian tried not to let it bother her, but it did. Was she too sensitive? Maybe it had nothing to do with her, but she doubted it.

"Dolly, I think I'll start on sewing a dress if that is fine with you."

Dolly smiled. "Of course, and if you need help most of the wives can sew. Clarissa, Donnell's wife, is so very talented. She makes the most beautiful lace. You could ask her."

"Thank you for your advice." Uncomfortable with so many eyes on her, she dipped her head down and ate. Conversation went on all around her, but she couldn't concentrate on what they were saying.

After supper she undertook the dishes and helped Dolly clean the kitchen. There was still plenty of light left, and she didn't want to keep Donald waiting.

"Dolly, what do you think of Donald Dill? Has he worked here long?"

Dolly gazed at her for a moment. "He's a good man. He's worked here since he was a boy. His pa died while he was young—he was about ten—and he started working here. He made sure his mother and sister never went without a roof over their heads or food on their table. He often asked if there was extra work he could do. Mr. Kavanagh paid him a man's wages. He told him he was doing a man's work, but he also needed to spend time on his ma's place."

"I'm glad to hear it."

"You planning to let him court you?"

Her face heated. "No, nothing like that. He's going to show me the horses. In fact, he's probably waiting for me now. I'll be back when it gets dark. That is, if it's fine with you."

"Go, have some fun for a change. I'll see you later." Dolly practically shooed her out of the house.

It was much cooler, and the crisp air contained a promise of an autumn to come. Excitement shot through her when she spotted Donald leaning against the corral fence. His smile upon seeing her brought her happiness. Walking faster, she reached him in no time.

"Good evening, Julian. You're a fine sight this day." He flashed her a heart-stopping grin.

Swallowing hard, she worked to act confident, but her blush probably gave her away. She wasn't fine, but it was nice to hear. "Are most of the horses in the pasture or in the barns?"

"We have a system," he stated as he held his arm out to her. She took it and they walked. "Injured horses are in. There are a few horses who refuse to be stalled. As long as they behave when ridden I find it not to be a problem. The brothers' horses are put in the barn each evening. I usually wait and to do it in the evening, so they have a chance to enjoy the pasture. Then there are mares who are almost ready to foal."

They reached the wooden fence that blocked off one side of the big pasture. "That sounds like a lot of horses."

He smiled. "I suppose it is. I'm just so used to having so many it doesn't seem like a lot to me."

She removed her hand from his arm. "Dolly told me a bit about you. I asked if you were a good man. She declared you were, and she told me you have a sister and mother you take care of."

He nodded. "My sister is married now and owns a house of her own. She has two wonderful boys. My ma still lives with me. She's getting older but insists on taking care of the chores herself; the cooking, cleaning, and laundry. Of course, she always discovers something that needs doing."

His face brightened when he spoke about his family. It was nice to watch.

"They don't make women any better than Dolly," he continued with a fond smile. "When I first arrived here, she wouldn't let me leave with empty hands. She always had a meal or a pie for me to bring home. It helped tremendously. We were able to get out from under a mountain of debt and back on our feet. That helped to calm my mother. She had a hard time after my pa died. What about you?"

She faced the fence and observed the horses. A few were rolling on their backs. "My family were poor sharecroppers. My pa scrimped, and we all went without so we could save every penny we could. My parents wanted a better life for me. The area we lived was cramped and men did what they wanted. I was dressed as a boy for as long as I can recall. Girls either went missing or they ended up so very broken. The law pretended the sharecroppers didn't exist unless they committed a crime closer to town. I remember happy loving times, but I also remember being hidden many times." She shifted and gave him a small smile. "Then Ma died, and my pa and I came here to buy a piece of land and livestock. My pa hurt his leg, and he died. Then I learned that we'd been swindled out of our money. Angus was nice enough to bring me here."

"I know the rest of the story, I believe." His eyes were full of understanding, and it melted her insides.

"Angus now owns the worthless little piece of land my pa purchased that I'd assumed belonged to me." A sad smile tugged at her lips. "I found out he's my guardian. I didn't have ill intentions but lying about being a boy was wrong. And now Angus will never forgive me."

"Hey, don't cry." He placed his arms around her and drew her close.

Gently, she pushed him and turned away. "Thank you. You are a good man, Donald. I appreciate you wanting to comfort me, but I don't want Angus to become upset with you too."

He took another step back. "You're right, it wouldn't be fitting seeing this is our first date and all."

A date? A candle of hope lit inside her. "I probably should have asked permission to see you, but he didn't join us for supper and I so wanted to visit the horses. I'm certain it's fine. If it isn't, he'll let us know."

"I expect he'll let us know any second now."

She twisted in the direction that Donald was looking, and sure enough Angus was almost upon them. She smiled. "Angus join us. I was just watching the horses. They are magnificent creatures." She turned back to the pasture.

"I was wondering where you had dashed off to."

Was he scolding her? She gazed at him and he was scowling. He *was* scolding her.

"There was no running involved. Dolly knew where I was, and you weren't around for me to ask your permission."

He nodded absently. "How'd the palomino do today?"

"He's got to be one of the best I've encountered in a while."

They talked about horses and ranch work. None of it included her. Angus had ruined any happiness she'd had. They didn't address her at all.

"Good night." She didn't wait for any answering words. She didn't want any. Angus easily dominated the whole conversation. When she was practically to the house, she started running until she was inside.

"Julian—"

"It was fine, Dolly. Good night." She retired to her room and put her nightgown on. Would Angus yell at her tomorrow? He was taking up too many of her thoughts, but she didn't know how to get him out of her head.

Sighing in frustration, Angus rolled onto his other side. Sleep wasn't coming at all. What did being a guardian entail? Was he expected to warn Donald off? Julian was old enough to be courted. He hadn't really spoken to her since she'd confessed to him. He still felt as though the rug was yanked out from under him.

How hadn't he seen? She was a pretty woman with smooth skin and soft eyes. Her hair still required work, but he should have noticed. She'd made a fool of him. He turned over again.

Why was he really mad? He shook his head. Part of it was his ego. She gotten the drop on him. Part of it was the lies. They had slept in the same bed, bathed in the pond at the same time! She should have told him before they washed. She must have realized just how inappropriate it was. Maybe she *was* trying to drag him to the altar.

He wouldn't allow that to happen. Did he have special

duties as guardian to a woman? She seemed comfortable with Donald.

He hadn't slept much the night before, speculating what to do, and he wasn't drawing closer to an answer.

Dolly was giving her a few chores. Maybe he should be the one telling her what to do. Part of the problem was he missed his buddy today. He'd enjoyed talking to Julian, the boy'd had so many questions. The delight on his face when he saw something new… She, she was a she. When *she* saw something new…

He couldn't avoid eating in the house forever. Somehow, he'd just have to act like she was a… how was he expected to be? After he mulled it over, he decided distant yet courteous would be the way.

Sun streamed into his room. He settled his arm over his eyes for a moment. Surprisingly, he'd slept. He felt energetic. Quickly, he dressed and went down the stairs. He stopped on the last step, watching as Julian looked to be having a lively discussion with Dolly and Gemma. She was getting on fine.

He stepped down and cleared his throat to alert them he was there, not wanting to eavesdrop. Both Dolly and Gemma turned and offered him a smile.

"Good morning, ladies." He stared at the back of Julian's head. It felt like blatant disrespect. "Julian, may I speak to you for a moment?" She spun, her eyes full of surprise.

She dried her hands and then walked over to him. "Yes?" She gazed up at him. She wasn't very tall. Julian the boy was supposed to have a growth spurt. Anger filled him.

"Did you hear me say good morning?"

She flushed and nodded.

"Yet you didn't return my greeting or look at me. You ignored me. I will not tolerate disrespect from my ward." Did those words just come from him? She was turning him into someone he didn't recognize… or like.

"Good Morning, Mr. Kavanagh."

"That's not humorous. My name is Angus. I could have expressed my anger in front of Dolly and Gemma, but I respect you so I'm telling you privately."

She swallowed hard and then stared at his boots. "I've never had a guardian. I'm sorry, Angus."

"Show me the same respect you'd give your pa."

Her eyes met his, flashing pain. "I need to help with breakfast…" Her chin quivered.

He nodded, feeling like a first-class jerk. He'd skip breakfast and take Captain up to one of the outer pastures. He wasn't her pa; he didn't want to be her pa. Why had he said such a thing?

CHAPTER ELEVEN

With a heavy heart, Julian went about her day. It was futile to try thinking of anything else but Angus. He'd been so different before she told him the truth. She was glad she wasn't lying anymore, but she must have hurt Angus.

Eventually, she ended up at the community garden. Brenna and Sheila were both picking vegetables for their suppers, chatting and laughing.

As she approached, they smiled at her. "Come, join us!" Sheila called out.

She walked to the other side of the garden and dropped to her knees. "It's a splendid garden. You all share it?"

Brenna nodded. "We all tend to it too. Sometimes when it is scorching hot out, it can be a challenge. How are you holding up? Angus wasn't at breakfast."

"It's not going well. Angus is furious with me. He's my guardian for ten more months, and I don't think my heart can take it."

Sheila reached out and patted Julian's arm. "Have you talked to him about it?"

"I haven't had enough of a chance. I haven't even apologized to him properly. This morning he told me I had to be respectful toward him." She glanced from one woman to the other. "I know little of the world. I've been a boy since I was nine. Wearing a dress is strange but pleasant. I'd been waiting for the day I could be just me. I'm a disaster."

Brenna tilted her head. "My suggestion would be to apologize to him. The Angus I know is easy going."

"He's due north if you want to see him," Sheila said with a bolstering smile.

Julian stood. "That would be a great place to start. Thank you both." She stood. "I'm hoping we can be friends."

Brenna waved her hand. "We already are."

Julian hurried to the barn before she talked herself out of going. No one was around. It would be near impossible to saddle Smokey, but she had to try. Smokey bobbed his head when he saw her.

"Ready for a ride?" she asked.

She carried the saddle to the stall and hoisted it onto the top of the stall wall. After she rested a bit, she was able to get Smokey saddled. Now for the bridle. Smokey practically walked right into it. Pleased, she led the horse to a table with tools on it. After climbing on the table, she hoisted herself onto the horse. Whew. It was draining work. Now to find Angus.

She'd never been useful with directions, but she was pretty sure she was going north. A cooling breeze felt wonderful. Her bonnet kept falling off and her hair was on end. Maybe one day she'd have hair like the other women; long, glossy, braided hair. Her mother'd had long hair that she'd put up in a bun. Pa would tease her as her hair came down piece by piece throughout the day. Oh, how she missed them.

A rider came into sight up ahead. Her heart skipped a

beat. Angus! When he turned and rode toward her, she wanted to whirl Smokey around and return to the ranch house. What was she expecting to say? The closer he got, the angrier he appeared. He stopped Captain in front of her.

His eyes narrowed as he stared at her. Why hadn't she fixed her bonnet?

"Why are you on that horse?"

"You gave me this horse." She held her voice light and matter of fact.

"I gave Julian the boy that horse. It's too much horse for a woman." He shook his head.

Getting kicked in the stomach would have hurt less. "I need to speak with you."

Angus quickly dismounted and lifted his arms up to help her down, but she'd already started to swing out of the saddle. They collided and ended up in a heap on the ground. Unfortunately, she'd been the one to break the fall.

There was a pointed rock under her back, and she shrieked. Angus pulled her up to a sitting position.

"And that is why I don't want you to have that horse."

"That horse has a name. We call him Smokey." She stopped talking. Angus' glare looked dangerous.

She stood and dusted herself off. She shouldn't have come looking for him. She'd go back to the ranch, but Smokey was too tall for her to get on. Taking his reins, she walked away. She'd find a rock or something.

"Get back here."

Her legs shook, but she managed to turn back around.

He glared at her again and then muttered something under his breath. "You're frightened of me." He looked dumbfounded. "Your nose is sun burned. Let's walk the horses to the trees. We can sit and talk. I won't hurt you; I promise."

Hesitating, she bit her lip. Did she have much choice?

Trusting him, she followed Angus to the trees. They both sat in the shade.

"Now, what was so urgent you had to ride all the way here?"

"I can't continue the way we are. You barely talk to me. In fact, most of the time you evade me. Angus, I'm very sorry I lied. I should have trusted you with the truth. I was apprehensive. My foolishness has cost me your friendship and it hurts so much, Angus."

"You carried your ruse too far when we cleaned up at the pond. I even tied myself to you as your guardian." He stared out at the grass.

A tear trail down her cheek. "What can I do to make matters right?"

"I don't think it will ever be the same as it was. I was very fond of the boy. Julian, you made a fool of me. I spent a lot of time with you and I never once guessed. What made you choose to be truthful?"

"God."

"God?"

"Yes, lying is a sin. The one lie turned into a mess of lies and that isn't how I wish to live my life. I want to be a normal person who people can trust. Honesty is God's way, at least I believe it to be. I know God forgives me. I hope you will too, someday." Looking at his pain-filled eyes was too extreme, and she turned away.

"That's it, I'm just expected to say everything is fine? Everything is unusual now. You're a female."

"Yes, one that still wants to learn how to ranch. You own my pa's place." She clasped and unclasped her hands. Everything was just so awkward.

"Yes, I do. Frankly, I don't know what I will do with it now. If I give it to you, you'll try to do all the work yourself."

"You'd rather I learn how to pour tea and make polite conversation."

"That is exactly what I was thinking. Eventually you'll want a husband and children, and I can't in good conscience let you continue doing men's work. I'm sorry, Julian, but that's just how things are."

His words shattered her. He hadn't listened to her. He discarded all she had learned from him.

"It's only until I'm twenty. I can hold out for ten months, and then you'll never have to give me another thought."

His brow furrowed. "I'm your guardian until you're married. It would have been twenty if you were a man but you're not. I know I told you twenty, but I checked with the lawyer and the change from being a guardian to a boy is drastically different than being a guardian to a female."

Could he do that? There wasn't anything more to say. She stood, adjusted her bonnet, grabbed Smokey's reins, and started walking back the way she had come. Why had she expected he'd come around? Her heart ached the most, she realized, because she loved him. Why hadn't she known how she felt until now?

She walked through the grass until she located a towering rock. She climbed it and got onto Smokey's saddle. She had chores to do, and then she needed to be alone to lick her wounds. She did not understand how to act anymore. No one had ever taught her.

Love? It wasn't worth the pain it created.

Angus couldn't find Julian when he returned home. If she had gone to the stream… He shuddered. Brenna had almost drowned not too long ago. He knocked on her bedroom door, doubting she was in there.

When the door opened, he was surprised but pleased.

Julian glanced at him and strode to her bed where sewing supplies were strewn. "Am I supposed to be someplace?" she asked in a stilted, wooden voice. "I had an early supper and Dolly said she'll let me know if she needs me when the dishes need to be washed." She kept her head down the entire time she spoke. Claws and her kittens were playing with the thread.

"I just wanted to know where you were. I'll…see you later." He stepped back and closed the door. Now what? She certainly was a moody one. It would probably be best to leave her alone. He groaned. He couldn't leave her alone, he was her guardian. Everything was in such a tangle.

But maybe he should let her be for a bit. He nodded, liking that idea. Yes, time would sort it all out.

At supper he merely shrugged when asked where she was.

"She's sewing a dress. She ate earlier so she could concentrate on that," Dolly explained.

"I'm helping with the dishes," Gemma said.

"No. That is Julian's job. She has to learn responsibility," Angus told her.

"It's your decision," Gemma said lightly.

Angus pushed back from the table. "Excuse me." He wasn't looking forward to chastising Julian, but he needed to set a pattern so they both knew what he expected of her. He hesitated and then knocked.

She answered, "Come in."

He opened the door and practically laughed. There were scraps of material all over the bed and the floor, along with a good amount of thread. "What took place in here?"

His amusement faded when she glared at him.

"I'm making a dress. Have you ever made your own clothes? Of course not. I made a few shirts for my pa, but dresses are different. I'm discouraged and about to tear my hair out, but I'm determined to figure this out myself. Claws, Paws and Jaws have been helping." She took a deep breath and as she let it out, it sounded as though she deflated. "Was there something you wanted?"

He almost gave her a break, but she needed to help with the chores. "You need to clean the dishes. You were absent at supper. You do know they are barn cats, right?"

"Yes, they only come in once in a while. Claws cries if she's inside too long. And I already told you that I took an early supper and Dolly said she would let me know when to come help clean," she snapped. Then, "Ouch," she cried then put her finger in her mouth.

He instantly went to her side and drew her hand in his. "Needle?"

She nodded as she gazed at him. Her eyes grew wet.

"I'm sorry." He rubbed her finger and gentled his voice, feeling contrite for his mulish behavior. "You don't have to help with the dishes." Being near her brought him warmth but touching her made him feel alive. Quickly he let go of her hand and stepped back to the door.

"I'll be right out to clean the dishes. It was important enough for you to come get me," she said, her voice was just above a whisper.

He went back to the dining table and took his seat. Staring at his plate, he furrowed his brow. "Why are you all staring at me?"

"I didn't mean to interfere, but I told her Gemma would more than likely help me with the dishes so she could sew her dress. I told her I'd let her know if I required her. I had no notion you'd be mad," Dolly said gently.

"I'm not mad. If she had your permission fine. Next time one of you has to let me know so I don't look like the bad guy. She needs routine and that consists of doing her chores."

From the corner of his eye, he caught Dolly and Gemma

exchanging a look. If he didn't know better, he would think those two were upset with him.

Julian appeared and quickly cleared the table without a word, though her face was a deep shade of crimson. What was with the women? What was he supposed to do? Structure and routine were what a young woman needed.

"How is the dress coming?" Dolly asked. She rubbed the length of Julian's arm.

It felt nice to have reassurance. Julian grinned at Dolly. "I'm getting the pieces cut. I'm sorry that I made things uncomfortable. I suppose I should have asked Angus if I could sew. I shouldn't have taken you up on the offer to have Gemma help you with the dishes. I'm not one to shirk my tasks. If I had we'd have starved long ago."

"You and Angus are finding your way. There are bound to be a few misunderstandings at the start. Ten months will pass by quickly, you'll see."

Julian's bottom lip wobbled. "I misunderstood the information about that. He's my guardian until I'm married."

Dolly's eyes widened. "I didn't know he could do that, but a woman does usually remain under her father's roof until she is married. I'm sorry, I know you're having a terrible time dealing with all of this and mourning your pa too."

Julian finally relaxed and completed the dishes. She needed to talk to Angus. She would just have to track him down, she supposed. Loud thumping from outside caught her attention, and she hastened to the front door. Upon spying Angus and Rafferty rolling around in the dirt punching each other, she flew outside and down the steps.

They stood and circled, and when they rushed at each other, she was in the middle. The next thing she realized, she was on the ground. Pain coursed through her head. She heard Teagan yelling for Dolly. Angus and Rafferty were busy pointing at one another and declaring it was the other's fault. Gemma, with her baby in her arms, dropped to her knees.

"Stop fighting right now!" Gemma pushed Julian's hair back and shook her head. "They got you good. You'll have a black eye for certain."

Angus gathered Julian up in his arms and carried her into the house and to her room. Rafferty, quick on their heels, hurried to the bed and swept all her dress pieces onto the floor so Angus could set her down.

"Don't you know not to get in the middle of a fight?" Angus sounded more worried than angry. That was a first.

"I—I didn't want Rafferty to injure you." She wished she could have answered it without her feelings showing.

"Out of the way, boys." Dolly wet a cloth in the basin of water she carried in and washed Julian's face. Dolly sure was gentle, but when she cleaned around Julia's right eye, the pain was a bit much.

Julian drew in a sharp breath as a spiking sensation shot through her skull.

Gemma handed a cup of tea to Angus. "Get her to drink this for the pain."

"Willow bark?"

She nodded, already leaving, cooing to the baby in her arms.

"We need to keep the wet cloth over your eye for a while. It should help with the swelling."

Angus set the teacup on the bedside table and helped her sit up. He carefully placed the cup of tea in her hands, and then he lifted the cloth from Dolly. "I think I can handle matters for a bit."

Oh, how she needed to tell him to just leave, but it

wouldn't be acceptable. Sipping her tea, her muscles relaxed. Her stomach still clenched, but that would go away when Angus left. He always caused some nervousness.

"Is the tea helping? I'm sorry Rafferty hit you. He strikes hard." He perched on the edge of the bed, gripping the wet cloth.

"He didn't punch me, you did."

The surprise on his face turned to horror, and finally he looked apologetic. "Are you certain?"

"Positive." She handed him the empty teacup and stared at him, fascinated.

"You shouldn't have jumped between us. I can hold my own against that young pup. You're probably right. If he had hit you, it wouldn't have been near as painful as my punch." He nodded.

"So, it's my fault?" She stared at her hands folded on top of the quilt. She was just trying to help. He never showed her anything but criticism. Her spirit plummeted. "The fight was about me, wasn't it?"

"Rafferty thinks he knows better how to be guardian to a girl. It was a difference of opinion. I would have won..." He leaned closer and peered at her. "Are you crying? Is it hurting more?"

"I don't need bruises to be hurt by you. Don't worry, I will try my best to find a husband and you'll be off the hook. One more thing. I'm a woman, not a girl. Maybe Rafferty doesn't like that you treat me like a disobedient child." Her hands shook.

"I'm sorry I hit you. I'm sorry it upset you but I'm doing right by you, and don't you dare get married without my permission." He handed her the wet cloth and strode out the door; his boots echoed down the hall.

Of course, it hurt. No one had ever hit her before. It was a poor decision to try to stop the fight. It seemed right at the time. Her feelings for that overbearing man were deeper than she'd thought. It had been too much to watch Rafferty hitting Angus. Angus might think he was winning, but he wasn't.

Dabbing the cloth around her eye, she winced. It didn't matter what she did, she did it wrong. He could have at least picked up her sewing from the floor. With a sigh, she lay back. She'd get it later, after the room ceased spinning.

CHAPTER TWELVE

There was no hurry in finding Julian a husband. She needed to learn about being female first. Angus shook his head. For the last four days she'd acted as though it was his fault she was stuck in bed. All she did was sew. Every time he stepped in to check on her, there she was with all that fabric scattered about her, needle in hand. And he didn't tell her it didn't look like any dress he'd seen before.

Rafferty wasn't talking to him. Did Rafferty care for Julian? Why else would he be mad? It was a situation he'd need to monitor. All the Julian worries had taken up all his free time. Her pa had done a good job raising a boy. Didn't he think she'd need to know how to run a household? An intriguing thought entered his mind. Maybe he needed to send her to finishing school?

He saddled Captain and rode into town. He needed a solution; he just wasn't sure what it was going to look like. After the relatively short ride, he pulled up at just the place he might find that solution and got off Captain. Then he tied the reins round the hitching post in front of the general store and went in.

The place was full of women, and that was what he needed, feminine advice. He stood and watched for a moment before he approached Mrs. Hutton. "Good Morning."

She turned and smiled. "Angus, how are you?"

"I'm well." He shifted his weight from one foot to the other. "Fact is, I need some advice. You've raised four well-mannered daughters."

"Yes, I have." Mrs. Hutton blushed.

"I need to find someone to teach my ward how to act proper."

Her eyes lit up. "Oh, I know just the person for you. Miss Cabot is the one you need. Fine manners, very fine manners, indeed. I've recommended her to everyone. She lives here in town. You know the house with all the roses in front? She lives there." Her lips curved into a pleasing smile. "Best of luck to you and your ward, Angus."

"Thank you, Mrs. Hutton. I'll be heading over to see Miss Cabot now."

He walked out of the store wondering why Mrs. Hutton had asked nothing about his ward. True, she'd attended church with the family, and revealing she was female instead of the boy he'd thought had raised some eyebrows. But Mrs. Hutton had behaved as though she had no questions, which was very unlike her. That was another thing he wanted Julian to learn, not to gossip.

He met with Miss Cabot, and they agreed to terms. He would send a buggy for her this afternoon. She looked like a schoolteacher. Hair pulled back so severely it was almost as though she hadn't any. She was tall and reed thin. She also wore glasses. She seemed to be a no-nonsense type of woman. Just what Julian needed.

He smiled all the way home. He was proud to make the right choices for Julian. He couldn't wait to tell her.

"No." Julian stared at him with her arms folded in front of her.

"I never said you had a choice. In fact, she'll be here shortly. She'll need a room to sleep in, so she can have mine. You'll get it ready for her and inform Dolly that we'll be having a guest for a few weeks."

"Weeks?" Maybe he'd hit his head.

"I'll be back when I hear the buggy."

"But—" The front door closed before she could say any more. She already knew how to cook and clean and take care of the house. She knew a lot about ranching and animals too. Somehow, he left her feeling like she wasn't enough. Why couldn't he just like her the way she was?

Sighing, she grabbed fresh linens and climbed the stairs. The scent that was Angus lingered in the room. Smelling the mix of fresh air, woods, and leather used to comfort her, but not anymore. She opened the window to air the room out. She then made the bed with clean sheets.

Dolly stopped at the door. "Did he tell you to change his sheets?" Her brow furrowed.

"No. He has a guest coming for a few weeks. Someone to teach me about manners, keeping house, and I guess how to be a woman." Her eyes grew wet, and she blinked back the tears. Her face was still bruised, but the swelling around her eye had gone down. Still, the motion stung some.

Dolly gave her a sad smile. "Maybe it'll be fun?"

Julian had known she would get no support from Dolly. Angus had already told Dolly to mind her own business. Did he not realize his words hurt? For Dolly's sake, Julian nodded. "Perhaps… Anyway, I'll try it. It might be fun."

Dolly nodded. "I best get things started in the kitchen."

"I'll be down to help when I finish." Julian watched Dolly

head to the stairs. Julian opened the window and stared out of it. She wished she'd never told him the truth. She should have just left. The buggy was coming up the drive. She was going to be sick, but she'd best be downstairs to greet the teacher.

She stood a few feet from the door with her hand over her stomach. She wasn't formerly educated, but her pa taught her a lot. He was always borrowing books, and they'd read many of the classics. He'd quiz her and teach her while they were out in the fields.

The door opened and a very stern looking woman stepped inside. Angus was right behind her.

"Miss Cabot, this is my ward, Julian."

"Julian what? What is her surname?" Miss Cabot seemed the impatient type.

"Field. This is Julian Field."

"Miss Field," Miss Cabot said as she studied her. The look on her face said it all. She'd been found lacking. "It's a pleasure to meet you."

Julian didn't know what to say, so she said nothing.

"The correct response would be, 'it's a pleasure to meet you too, Miss Cabot.'"

Julian nodded.

"Miss Field, please greet me properly," Miss Cabot said.

"It's a pleasure to meet you too, Miss Cabot."

"Very good. I think we'll get along splendidly."

"I'm Dolly," yelled the housekeeper from across the room. "As long as you don't correct me in any way we'll get along splendidly too."

Miss Cabot gave her the barest of nods.

"I can make tea," Dolly shouted.

"Thank you that would be most delightful, I'm sure, but I'd prefer water for Miss Field and myself." Miss Cabot handed her gloves, hat, and wrap to Angus.

"If you'd prefer coffee—" Dolly offered.

"Water is better. Tea and coffee are full of stimulants that are not proper for a young lady, not to mention the detriment to the hair and teeth." Miss Cabot turned to Angus. "I will teach Miss Field how to complete a coffee or tea service. So many like to drink them when they visit."

What visitors? They were all family. Angus' warm gaze was upon her, she could feel it. Summoning a pretend smile, she glanced at him. It was hard to control her instinct to run to her room and close the door.

"Let me show you to your room, Miss Cabot," Dolly said. She didn't wait for an answer, she just went up the stairs.

Miss Cabot gave Angus a regal nod before she followed.

"Angus, what in the world?" demanded Julian when Miss Cabot had disappeared up the stairs.

"I'm doing right by you, Julian. Knowing manners and things will make you very marriageable. You'll have a better option of husbands. I expect you to obey Miss Cabot." Angus grabbed his hat and left.

The Angus she'd first known had been a kind, understanding man. Now he seemed neither. He left that prune of a woman in charge of her? Her manners must have been deplorable in his eyes. She'd try hard to learn, and maybe Angus wouldn't be ashamed of her. She might even make him proud. That would be a refreshing change. He'd always been so pleased and proud when he'd believed she was a boy.

Dolly came down first, shaking her head and mumbling, "I'll get you both water."

"Dolly, I don't want you to have to do anything extra."

"Don't you worry none. I don't plan to. I might be grouchy, though. Just remember, it's not because of you." She marched toward the kitchen, still shaking her head.

"Come, Miss Field," Miss Cabot commanded as soon as she came down the stairs. "Let's enjoy a pleasant glass of water." She walked ahead, expecting Julian to follow. She moved to one of the upholstered chairs near the fireplace. Slowly, she perched on the edge of the seat.

Women are supposed to sit that way? There must be a lot she didn't understand. Julian sat slowly in the chair opposite. She tried to sit on the edge of her chair, but she almost hit the floor instead. She'd have to practice.

"I understand both your parents are deceased. You weren't taught gentility. Luckily, I am here. There is much to learn." Dolly set two glasses of water on the table between them and left. Miss Cabot frowned. "I will take every opportunity as a learning lesson. One never carries filled glasses. The glasses are to be empty and a pitcher filled with water should be brought also on a tray. First, you will set the glass down and then carefully pour the water into the glass. After the glasses are filled, you then set the pitcher close to the hostess."

"Yes, Miss Cabot. The hostess is who?"

"The hostess is the woman who the guests came to visit. Sometimes if there is more than one female, then you defer to the eldest."

Julian nodded. What did defer mean? She wasn't about to ask.

Gemma came inside with her baby. "Hello." She sat on the sofa and nursed the baby.

Miss Cabot stiffened and frowned. What was she frowning at? Julian set her glass down as quietly as she could.

"Excuse us," Miss Cabot snipped. "We will resume lessons on the front porch." She stood so straight and tall. "Come along, Miss Field."

CHAPTER THIRTEEN

*A*ngus sat at the table waiting for supper. Everyone was quiet, too quiet, and the tension was high. Glancing around, he received glares from everyone except Julian and Miss Cabot. Now what? He'd had an aggravating day pulling a calf out of mud only to find the mother refused to nurse him. He went from cow to cow with the calf and sure enough the calf was adopted and allowed to nurse. That cow's calf looked to be missing. Could be dead.

Gemma had an expression on her face as though she wanted to strangle him. What had transpired?

"Miss Cabot, how are things working out so far?" he inquired.

She set her fork down and wiped her mouth before speaking. "It's always an adjustment for the household the first day. You must realize I am teaching Miss Field not only manners but how to enter society. When I am done, she will easily be able to socialize with the upper crust. I'm certain she'll make a wonderful match and live a life of high society."

"Very good." That was what he wished, wasn't it? He

wanted her to make the best potential match. "Miss Field, are you listening carefully and learning what you should?"

Julian turned a bright shade of red. He expected a nod, but she put her fork down, wiped her mouth before she spoke.

"I am learning a lot. Of course, much of what I learn I will have to practice. Thank you for asking—" Confusion crossed her face. "What do I call him?"

"You shall address him as sir, or perhaps Uncle Angus? We'll get that straightened out as soon as I figure out the entire family structure."

Angus sputtered his coffee into his napkin. Uncle, Uncle Angus? He wasn't sure if he should agree or laugh. "I like being called sir. The other I must think about. She is my ward, but we're not related."

"May I suggest Mr. Angus? It is acceptably formal without being too formal. As her ward you are raising her. Miss Field must always show respect. We will work on it."

His gaze met Teagan's as his brother's lips twitched. The door opened and Rafferty strolled in.

"Glad I didn't miss supper. I'm starved." His chair made a loud scraping sound as he slid it out. He plopped down and pulled himself up to the table with more scraping. Without waiting for anyone else, he picked up his spoon and began slurping the thick beef stew in front of him.

Miss Cabot flinched at the sound and subjected Angus' brother to a harsh stare.

Glancing up, he blinked. "Whoa there. I know you're here to teach Julian how to act and all but don't think I want to learn a thing. I'm Rafferty, the good son."

Teagan lost his battle with merriment. He roared with laughter until he rose and flew out the back door. Angus still heard his guffaws after the door was closed.

"It's nice to meet you Rafferty. I am Miss Cabot, and yes I am here to teach Miss Field." She went back to eating.

"Your last name is Field?" asked Rafferty. "I guess I never asked before. Enjoying your lessons?"

"Yes, sir, I am." This time she kept her head down.

"Miss Field when we speak, we raise our chin so those with whom we are conversing can hear us. It's only polite to look at the person you are addressing."

"Humph," Dolly muttered.

Rafferty glared at him. "I've never observed bad manners from Julian."

Julian's eyes filled with pain. "My guardian would prefer for me to be marriageable. I believe Mr. Angus wants me settled as swiftly as possible."

Angus opened his mouth, closed it, and then opened it again. "I want to be sure you attract a man with excellent qualities."

"What exactly are these 'qualities'?" Rafferty cocked his brow.

"Educated, honorable, and a gentleman who is a part of society."

Rafferty's eyes filled with mirth. "We are the society. If you're talking about the snobs who think they run the town, truly I'd hate for Julian to get caught up in all that."

Miss Cabot's eyes glittered. "Why would that be, Mr. Kavanagh?"

Rafferty shook his head before he pushed back from the table. "Thank you, Dolly. Supper was good." He dashed out the front door.

Angus smiled. "Miss Cabot, I should have anticipated resistance from my brothers. I apologize."

"It's no reflection on your fine character, Mr. Kavanagh." Miss Cabot remarked.

"If you'll excuse me, I'm to help Dolly wash the dishes."

Dolly waved her away. "You don't need to, honey."

"Learning to cook and clean are excellent lessons," Miss Cabot added.

Julian glanced at Angus, and he nodded to her. She stood and cleared the table. Her willingness to learn pleased him. "If you'll excuse me, I have some paperwork to do." He stood and went toward the office.

He hadn't expected such resistance from his brothers. What was wrong with doing the right thing? They didn't have daughters old enough for them to worry about. Rafferty might be right about the snobs. Angus would have to give that further consideration. But that would not stop the lessons.

He heard the Claws crying in Julian's room. He snuck her and her kittens outside before Miss Cabot saw them. He shook his head as he went into the office.

CHAPTER FOURTEEN

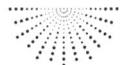

*J*ulian frowned when Miss Cabot handed her a hairbrush. "How many times?"

"You need to brush your hair one hundred times. It'll help with the growth. Tomorrow we'll make a hair wash from honey that is most excellent in thickening hair. Now brush your hair like I taught you. Then it's to bed with you."

"It's not late enough to go to bed," Julian protested.

"Retiring early and waking early will work wonders for your health, it'll make your skin softer. You see your body needs more rest to do all the wonders it does. A well-rested woman is the best kind. Good night."

"Good night, Miss Cabot." Julian waited until her door was closed before she put her head in her hands. How shameful to know nothing? When Miss Cabot told her they'd need to start from scratch, she wanted to weep. Would she ever be the women Angus expected her to be? She must be such a disappointment to him.

She sniffled. She'd work as hard as she could. Angus' approval meant so much to her. Maybe it was too much. A step back from him would be a step in the right direction. He wanted to be rid of her, and she didn't have any option; she had to respect his wishes.

Would she marry a man who lived in town? It would break her heart if she couldn't be near animals and land. Perhaps there was another rancher who needed a good wife. A cloud of sadness settled over her. She apparently wouldn't get to choose.

Lord, thank You for everything. I want for nothing because of You. Please help me learn how to be a good wife. I'd like to learn quickly, Lord. If You send the right man to be my husband, it would mean the world to me. Bless everyone here at the ranch, and I hope my pa has found my ma up there in heaven. I'm so glad my pa taught me about the Bible and praying. It's a special feeling to know I'm not alone; You are always with me. Good night.

Frustrated by the whole situation, she couldn't sleep, so she lit her oil lamp and sewed. Her dress was nearly done, and it was by far the finest thing she'd ever sewn. It was made of green and blue material. She especially liked the ruffles she'd added, plus the bows.

There'd been so much tension in the house, and it was all because of her. After church tomorrow, she'd probably have to find honey to make the fancy hair wash Miss Cabot mentioned. She shuddered. Her scalp already hurt from brushing her hair one hundred times. But the faster she learned; the faster Miss Cabot could disappear.

There, all done. She snipped a few threads from the dress and hung it up. She'd best get some sleep, so she would look well-rested.

ANGUS WATCHED, bewildered as Julian ate a hurried breakfast and apologized, telling him she wanted to put on her new dress for church. It surprised him Miss Cabot didn't correct her.

"Are you joining us, Miss Cabot?" he asked.

"No, you go ahead." She glanced away.

He studied her for a moment. "Do you believe in God?"

"I stopped for a while and I'm making my way back to Him. I'm not ready for church, though. Don't worry about me, I'm just fine."

Her fake smile didn't sit well with him. But he supposed it wasn't his business.

"I'll just get out of everyone's way and retire for a bit in my room," announced Miss Cabot.

He nodded and sipped his coffee. It was actually quiet in the house. Usually there were little ones running around shrieking or crying. This was peaceful. Sometimes quiet could be nice. He stood and turned when he heard Julian's footsteps coming down the hall. He held on desperately to his smile as he inwardly groaned.

Her gaze met his and she turned crimson. "What do you think?" Her eyes were as bright as her smile.

He didn't know what to say. The dress had ruffles striped across it, starting at her neckline. The bows dotting her skirt were… "You made that yourself?" He kept his smile.

"Yes! I'm so excited, Mr. Angus." She twirled around, obviously happy with her creation. When she stopped, he noticed the dress seemed to list to the left. The whole left side was longer than the right.

Dolly walked in and her mouth opened. Angus gave her a stare, hoping she'd fix everything.

"Oh look at you! You put a lot of hard work into your festive dress. It looks like you mastered sewing ruffles. Good for you."

Julian beamed. "I need to get the bonnet I made to match. Please excuse me while I get it."

Teagan took one glance and walked out the door, his laugh carrying loudly.

"Are we ready?" Gemma asked. She looked very nice in her plain blue dress.

Julian came running out with her ruffled bonnet. "I'm ready!"

He didn't have the heart to scold her for running. They all got into a wagon. Angus ended up sitting in the wagon's bed, where the "boy" Julian had sat on the occasions they had not ridden on horseback. He tried to get Dolly to meet his gaze, but she was avoiding him. She would not be any help. Gemma hadn't even mentioned the dress.

He couldn't allow her to walk into church wearing that monstrosity. She'd be gossiped about and that wouldn't do. They pulled up in front of the church and he still hadn't figured out what to say to her. Teagan and Gemma retrieved their children first. Then Angus helped Dolly down. "Be careful of the mud," he warned her.

He held his arms up to Julian. She still had stars in her eyes. *It's for her own good.* He swept her up, pretended to trip, and dropped her into the mud.

"Oh! Oh, look, my dress is full of mud! Does anyone have a handkerchief?" Tears shimmered in her eyes.

Confusion and sorrow filled him. He'd been trying to *prevent* tears.

Dolly stood just beyond the mud. "I'm so sorry, Julian. A handkerchief would only rub it in. Angus, go help her out of that mud and take her home."

"I'll come back with the wagon."

"We'll make do with the others," Teagan said. He gave Angus a look of understanding.

Julian sat on the front bench, trying to not feel. It would be easier if she could just turn to stone. Everything seemed to come at her, and she didn't want any additional pain. She removed her splattered bonnet and stared straight ahead. It wasn't Angus' fault.

"I think maybe it happened because of my sin of pride," she told him softly. "I was so proud of this dress, and the Lord teaches us to be humble. I may have to remove a few bows so it isn't so pretty. I wish I could find a middle spot where I'm not sinning all the time. I wonder what it would be like to be a reverend's wife. He'd probably be able to guide a person so they would end up in heaven. I just want to sob but I don't think that's allowed either."

"Crying isn't allowed?"

She shrugged her shoulders then cringed. "Oh, I forgot. Shrugging is bad too."

"It wouldn't be the end of the world if you broke a few of Miss Cabot's rules." Angus spoke in a gentle tone. "You've only spent one day with her. Sometimes, if we practice enough, things come naturally to us."

She gave him a sidelong look. "Maybe you're right. She will be mighty upset when she sees me. If I had clothes with me, I'd just dive in the pond." A smile played at the corners of her mouth. "You'd have to turn around and not see me."

"Of course."

"Angus? Is it hard?"

"Is what hard?"

"Is it hard to learn to be good? I'm not learning fast enough, and I think I'm just wasting Miss Cabot's time." She took the handkerchief he finally offered and dabbed her tears.

"You're doing just fine, honey." He reined in the horses. "Stay right where you are, I will change into some work clothes, put water on to heat for a bath, and come get you."

She nodded. How could he not think of her as pathetic? It was no wonder he preferred the notion of her being married and out of his way. How could she strengthen herself, and not feel so much?

"Angus, do you think I could visit Pa's grave?"

"Sure, honey. I'll take you tomorrow."

HE JUMPED DOWN and hustled into the house. His clothes weren't the cleanest, but they were nothing like Julian's. Remorse filled him for the deceit he'd pulled. After quickly changing, he put water on to heat. A lot of it. Next, he ran into her room and snatched her night gown. It would be the easiest. He stopped and opened a closet door where they kept linens and grabbed a stack of towels.

He heard what sounded like something falling in the office, but there wasn't time to investigate. He dropped his armload in the kitchen, fetched the tub and carried it into the kitchen before he went back outside.

She bore the most forlorn expression on her face, and it was all his doing. It would have been worse if he'd allowed her to walk into church, though. But how could he tell her? She smiled at him, stood and then leaned forward, and he swung her easily to the ground.

"I thought maybe we could sit out back while the water heats. I'll see if I can find Miss Cabot to help you. It would be a chore for you to get undressed yourself." He helped her to sit down. "I wager that dress is heavy on you. It felt like you'd gained at least twenty pounds when I lifted you down."

She flinched, and he wished he didn't have such a big mouth. "I didn't mean that you yourself had gained—"

This time she chuckled. "I understand, Angus."

The back door opened. "That should be Mr. Angus," Miss

Cabot corrected. Her eyes narrowed as she glanced from one to the other. "What happened? And where did you get that inappropriate dress?"

Angus gave her his best glare, but she ignored him.

"Inappropriate?" Julian's lower lip trembled.

"It's fine," he insisted and glared again, only to be ignored, again.

"Mr. Angus would you be so kind as to pour the water into the tub and then make yourself scarce. Also, be sure no cowboys drift this way."

He nodded. His glare had stopped people in their tracks, yet that thin woman pretended she didn't see it. The woman was abrasive and unsettling, but he still thought it advantageous for Julian to learn as much as she could. It was a genuine opportunity for her. It wouldn't be but for a few more weeks. "Miss Field, you're in excellent hands. I will see you later."

CHAPTER FIFTEEN

After supper, Dolly hung the dress to dry. "It'll be easier to brush off the mud and then wash it." Dolly turned and hugged Julian. "It's been a trying day for you."

Julian relished the affection. And her eyes were moist when the embrace ended. "Thank you, Dolly."

"I'd best get you back to Miss Cabot. I wonder if it hurts to have one's hair pulled so tight."

Julian put her hand over her mouth to keep from laughing. "I think it must."

Dolly smiled at her. She opened the back door and gestured for Julian to go first. As soon as they were inside they were being frowned at by Miss Cabot.

"When there are two women, it is proper to allow the eldest to walk through the door first."

"Yes, ma'am." Julian responded. Dolly walked past Miss Cabot without acknowledging her.

"Let's sit by the fireplace and we can have a talk," said Miss Cabot to Julian, leading the way.

Julian tried to stand straight and tall as she followed.

Miss Cabot settled herself on the sofa, gesturing for Julian to sit next to her. "Let's discuss your dress. It wasn't appropriate to wear to church. In fact, I can't imagine where you would wear such a dress except for the grandest of balls in England. Here in America it is poor manners to wear a dress that draws too much attention to the wearer. It is ostentatious."

"Miss Cabot, I don't exactly understand."

"When you call attention to yourself it shows that you have no regard for others. People—and I will say it is mostly women—tend to frown on such actions. It is fine to be self-confident and have an unusual dress. If you bring too much attention to yourself other young ladies will think you selfish in trying to draw the attention of all the best marriageable men. Conceited women are intolerable and are soon left off guest lists. I know you aren't that type of young lady, and I'd hate for others to make judgments due to one dress. People can be quick to judge. When you are a polite, kind woman you might not be noticed right away, but that is to your benefit. Patience is the key. You don't approach a man; the man approaches you. Do you understand what I'm saying?"

"Yes, I do. Be your best and be patient. Don't make it so everyone stares at you."

Miss Cabot smiled widely. "You are a smart pupil. Many young women struggle because they want to be the envy of all, but in the end these young ladies are not paid attention to or invited to events."

Angus came down the stairs. "How is she doing?"

"I was just telling Miss Field she is a star pupil. You should feel proud of your ward."

Angus gave them a regal nod that could rival Miss Cabot's. "I am very proud." He turned down the hall.

"Tomorrow we will get the honey for your hair. One day it will be long, thick, and shiny. Now I am going to my room to relax before bed. I suggest you read. A well-read lady is always an asset. I noticed many books in the office. You should pick one. Good night, Miss Field."

"Good night, Miss Cabot."

A soft knocking on the front door drew her attention, and she answered it. She smiled when she saw Donald. "Hello."

He smiled back. He had his hat in his hand. "I was wondering if you'd like to take a walk with me, Julian?"

"Let me get my wrap." She took it from a peg on the wall and drew it around her. She walked out to Donald, closing the door behind her.

A strong wind blew as they walked to the pasture fence. Julian pulled her wrap tighter. She shouldn't be out here and she'd hear about it from Miss Cabot, but she needed to be herself for just a few minutes.

"How are things with Miss Cabot?" Donald asked as he caught her gaze.

"Does everyone know about my lessons in manners?" Her face heated. Did they all look at her as some wild, unmannered girl?

"Most, I suspect. No one has mentioned your manners, but Miss Cabot has ruffled a few feathers on the ranch. I think most just want her to leave. Do you like her?"

"She has treated me with respect, mostly. She genuinely wants to teach me, and I've been trying my hardest except for right now. Walks with men at night are scandalous. Miss Cabot and Angus are determined I will marry a society man. Are there many around?" She sighed and watched the horses. The darker it got, the less active the horses were. Some had folded their legs and dropped to the ground.

"There are a few but I don't know them. I see Angus on the porch. I'd best walk you home. I hope I didn't cause you any trouble." He was a sweet, sincere man.

"Thank you, yes I need to go back." She took Donald's arm and they walked the short way to the house. He left her at the bottom of the stairs with a slight squeeze to her hand.

"Did you enjoy your walk?" Angus asked. The lantern light bathed his face, exposing his disappointment.

She climbed the three steps and stood before him. "It was nice to escape the troubles of today for a little while. I should have asked you."

"I take it Miss Cabot doesn't know?"

She shook her head. "Not unless she was watching out the window. Early to bed and all. I was supposed to go to the library and find a book to read. She likes your selection."

He smiled. "We'd best go find you a book. Maybe you can avoid being in her bad graces." He paused and drew a long breath. "Donald is a fine man."

Warmth suffused her face. "He's been nice to me. He's a friend. Let's go find a book. I need to get lots of sleep or I'll wake up old and wrinkled."

Angus chuckled. "We usually keep early enough hours. I thought the upper crust went to balls at night and then slept until the afternoon," he teased.

"I wouldn't know." They walked down the hall to the office. Angus opened the door for her and she entered the room, amazed by the number of books on the shelves. She'd never taken note of them before.

"Here is one that Gemma just finished. She enjoyed it." Angus handed her a book titled Eight Cousins by Louisa May Alcott.

"Written by a woman? I've heard about Treasure Island and Moby Dick, written by men." She laughed. "This looks wonderful, thank you." Their gazes met and all she could see was home. Angus had become her home. How did that happen?

"Good night." He glanced around as he saw her to the

door. "I heard something fall in here earlier and I want to see what it was. I'll see you in the morning and we'll go visit your pa's grave."

"Thank you. Good night Angus." Clutching the book to her chest, she hurried to her room.

THE NEXT MORNING, Miss Cabot frowned at her and shook her head. "Mr. Kavanagh, may I speak with you privately."

"Of course," he said with a nod.

They left Julian to feel like an errant child. She wasn't a child, but they acted as though she was very young.

"Julian what's wrong? Are those tears?" Dolly asked upon coming into the room.

"Mr. Angus and Miss Cabot are having a private discussion about me. I'm beginning to think I do nothing right. I took a short walk with Donald last night." She hung her head and she squeezed her eyes shut.

"Angus needs to take a step back and see what is happening. I am glad that he is taking his duties as a guardian seriously. He's not the most trusting of souls but win him over and he's the most loyal friend you'll ever have." She gave one of her kind smiles. "Do you want me to talk to him?"

Julian sighed and shook her head. "I have to take care of it myself. I appreciate the offer, Dolly. You have been so good to me."

"You just remember, there is much more right with you than not right. In fact, I don't know about all this gentility stuff. I never raised girls before."

Julian gave Dolly a sad smile. "I just want Angus to be proud of me."

"He already is—"

Miss Cabot came through the door first, followed by

Angus. She glided over and sat on the sofa next to Julian. Angus sat in a chair.

"Julian, I can't emphasize enough about propriety. It won't do for you to be outside in the dark with a man other than your guardian. It's for your safety as well as your reputation. Men marry women who are chaste, not women who are out at night." Miss Cabot's voice seemed louder than usual.

"I'm sorry."

"Julian, tell your guardian your sorry. He has the responsibility of you. What you do reflects on his reputation as well."

Her heart dropped as she gazed at Angus. "I'm so sorry, Mr. Angus. I'm lucky to have you. I'm lucky to have a roof over my head and food to eat. All I want is a home, and you provide it for me, but I realize you'd rather I marry so someone else can provide for me. I'll work harder and faster so there is no chance for your reputation to suffer." Tears poured down her face despite her fight to keep them at bay.

"A handkerchief is something you will want to have with you at all times," Miss Cabot instructed.

"Yes, Miss Cabot."

"Julian, you need to look at the person you're addressing," Miss Cabot reminded her.

Julian's face flamed. She'd disappointed Angus, and she couldn't seem to do anything right.

"Mr. Angus, I know we were going to see my pa's grave today, and I hope you don't think me rude, but I'd rather go another day if that is fine with you. I hope you didn't go to any trouble." She made her voice as emotionless as possible. If she went today, she'd just weep and weep. What if she couldn't stop? To keep her hands from trembling, she clasped them together and put them in her lap. There was no advantage to being a woman. What happened to her happiness or her spirit?

"It's fine, Julian. We can go another day. If you'll excuse me, I have work to do." When he walked away, it was as though he took her heart with him.

CHAPTER SIXTEEN

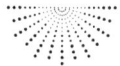

"Julian, tell me about your young man," Miss Cabot insisted.

"Do you mean Donald?"

Miss Cabot pursed her lips. "We do not use Christian names of men who are not related to us. What is his surname?"

"Dill," Julian responded as she furrowed her brow.

"You shall address him as Mr. Dill, never Donald. Using a first name suggests familiarity and it is not to your advantage to do so. Always converse with dignified modesty and simplicity. Sometimes the less said the better. We never talk about anything personal, such as what you or your family does. You must never appear to be smarter than the man who is leading the conversation. Being deceptive is never a choice, and we do not speak ill of any person. Gossip leads to trouble and embarrassment. It will highlight you as a person who is unwelcome."

Julian frowned. "What am I supposed to talk about?"

"The weather is always a safe subject. Now to address

your late-night frolic. You cannot be alone with a man who isn't related to you. You need to be chaperoned. Now, had you asked Mr. Angus, he could have watched you from the front porch."

"Miss Cabot, Mr. Angus was on the front porch, and I believe you were watching from the bedroom window." Julian lifted her chin.

"Miss Field, you are being disrespectful. It is none of your business what I was doing, and to make assumptions is simply not done. Assumptions only lead to trouble. Now let's work on the way you walk, shall we?"

"What is wrong with the way I walk?" Julian asked in dismay.

"Your stride is as long as a man's. Your shoulders are often hunched. One needs a straight spine and her head held high. Small steps are the steps of a proper woman."

For the next hour, Julian was made to walk back and forth until she was passable. Her face hurt from having to smile. She'd always managed to keep up with her pa from an early age. Shorter, slower steps made little sense. Wouldn't it just take her longer to get where she was going? There was too much to know and her head was spinning with useless information.

"Let's take a break. You've done remarkably well today."

As much as she didn't care for Miss Cabot, her praise was welcome. Julian still needed to brush out her dress and then wash it. It would be a lot of work, but it was worth it. She'd have to be careful of the bows and the ruffles. Perhaps she could cut the bows off and reattach them later. Then she would just have to be careful with the ruffles. There would be an opportunity to wear her dress, she just knew it. The next dress she made would be elegant and appropriate for church.

What would happen when Miss Cabot was finished? Would Angus prance her around like a new pony to see who was interested? She'd been wrong to fixate on Angus, but he had been her rock. A frown tightened her brow. Apparently, she needed to find a new rock. Maybe she didn't need one. Her heart hurt from grieving and all this, but perhaps if she kept to herself she could protect herself from shattering.

She grabbed a stiff brush and a pair of scissors on her way to the back yard. The mud on her dress had dried and there was so much of it. She gently cut off the bows and set them aside. She'd need to wash them too. She laughed as the cats each took one in their mouths and began to play. Taking the brush, she carefully brushed the mud off the dress. If the dress hadn't been so special to her she might not have bothered to take so much time on it.

"Howdy, Julian," Rafferty greeted as he rounded the corner to where she stood. He laughed. "I'm glad you finally realized that dress is used best as a rag. Imagine bows and whatever else you called those scrunchy strips. Who was the brave one to tell you?" He stood there with the ends of his lips tipped up.

Blood pounded in her ears. Her stomach rolled. She needed to be sick. Everyone thought her dress was best used as a rag? "You, Rafferty," she choked out. "You are the brave soul." She left the brush and scissors on the wooden table. Her dress slipped out of her hands and pooled on the ground. Angus had been right. She knew nothing. It was probably a good thing she had fallen in the mud or she would have shamed the entire family. Quickly, she ran to the side of the house and was promptly sick. At least she had a handkerchief to wipe her mouth with.

Beads of sweat formed on her brow, and her legs felt wobbly. She wanted to fall to the ground and sob, but somehow she managed to stay on her feet. Taking a deep breath, she went to the front of the house and then inside. She couldn't face Rafferty. Once in her room, she removed her dress and quickly put her boy clothes on. At least these felt normal. After waiting until she felt stronger, she left. There was one place where she'd be able to find solace.

Miss Cabot sat on the sofa sipping water. Dolly looked to be busy in the kitchen. Angus walked toward the kitchen. "Where is Julian?"

Dolly quickly glanced up at him. "I don't know. I thought she was with you."

He turned to Miss Cabot. "Where is she?"

"I haven't seen her this afternoon. I, like Dolly, thought she was with you."

He mumbled under his breath. "No one has looked for her?" He scowled and headed for her room. He knocked on the door and when he didn't hear any answer, he opened the door and peeked in. Then he walked in since it was empty. Where was she? The dress she'd worn that morning was on her bed, and her shoes were on the floor. He knew immediately what she'd done. She was pretending to be a boy again.

When he caught up with her he would… He huffed out a frustrated sigh. What was he supposed to do? Hopefully, he'd be cool headed when he found her. Without stopping to talk to Dolly or Miss Cabot, he stormed out the door and ran to the barn.

"Where is Donald?" He glanced from Shea to Rafferty.

"He's at the corral in the back," Shea told him. "What—" Angus didn't hear Shea's question. He strode out back, wanting nothing more than to hit Donald.

"Where is she?" he asked the ranch hand.

"Who?" Donald frowned and shook his head. "Julian? I haven't seen her since last night. Why? What happened?"

Angus took a deep breath and tried to calm himself before he hit the wrong person. "I don't know what happened, but I think she's wearing trousers again. I can't think what had set her off."

Rafferty slowly approached. "I know what it was, and before you punch me, I didn't know. I thought you'd told her or Miss Cabot had. She was in the back yard and I just wanted to say hello. She was cutting the bows off her dress—"

"Get to the end, Rafferty!" ground out Angus.

"I think I told her everyone would be happy to see she intended to use the dress as a rag. She paled a bit, and I think she might have vomited."

"Might have?"

"She went to the side of the house, and I heard her being sick." His brother shrugged. "I'm sorry."

It took everything he had to rein in his temper. "Do you know where she went after that?"

Rafferty shook his head. "I think she went inside. I'm sorry."

Angus frowned. "You can tell her that after I find her. Rafferty, please start thinking before you speak!"

He walked back into the barn and found that Shea had Captain saddled and ready to go.

"Find her and bring her home," Shea said softly.

Angus nodded and rode off. He had a good idea where she had gone. His heart hurt for her. She'd thought her dress to be pretty, and she was proud of her accomplishment. He couldn't think of her pain just now. He needed to concentrate on getting to her.

Just as he thought, she was at her pa's grave. She was on her knees and her body racked with sobs. Sorrow and a bit of shame unfurled in his gut and spread outward. This was his fault. She was shy and quiet, and he'd put her in a situation where the attention was on her. He'd allowed his family to see her faults, which weren't really faults. After he reined Captain in, he walked to her.

He dropped to his knees and gathered her in his arms. She was shaking and sobbing, and he was helpless to know what to do. He rubbed her back as he held her.

"I'm so sorry, Julian. You are perfect just the way you are. I set out to change you, and that wasn't right." He rocked her, and her sobs were like small knives going through him. In his quest to do right by her, he'd hurt her. He'd never heard weeping so deep before.

It was a long time before her body stilled. Her shoulders slumped as though she was exhausted.

"Are you all right?" he asked gently. "I'm so sorry, Julian."

She pulled away and stared into his eyes. "You have nothing to be sorry for, Angus. I'm the one who is uneducated in too many things. I've been nothing but an embarrassment to you. I don't want to marry into society. I want to stay right here." She swallowed hard.

"I can't leave you here, Julian. It wouldn't be right. My brothers would tar and feather me, not to mention Dolly. I'm sorry."

She glanced away. "It's because I'm female. If I was a man, you wouldn't think twice."

"Honey, that's just the way things are. As soon as word got out you were here alone, there'd be all kinds of strangers stopping by to visit. More than likely you'd end up dead. I couldn't bear for that to happen." He shifted to gaze into her eyes. "I'll send Miss Cabot on her way. You've learned more than you need."

"Thank you," she whispered. She stared at her pa's grave

for a time. "You dropped me in the mud on purpose, didn't you?"

Shocked, he didn't know what to say. But he expected folks to tell him the truth, so he wouldn't lie to her. "I did, and I apologize—"

"It is only useful as a rag!"

"I never said that. It just wouldn't have fit in. Maybe at a big party, but not at church. I didn't want the gossips to have something new to talk about." He brushed a strand of hair from her eyes. "I should have been honest with you, but I didn't want to hurt your feelings. It's a pretty dress and I'm sure if you lived in a big city, you'd wear it often to parties and weddings, but people here are simpler."

Nodding, she swallowed hard. "I just wanted to make you proud. I don't know why exactly but your opinion is important to me. I suppose you've taken up where my pa left off."

Like her pa? That brought a frown to Angus' forehead. He didn't have *fatherly* feelings for her. He sighed. He'd have to wait. Maybe it wasn't meant to be. After all, guardians didn't wed their wards. *Wed?* He needed to reel his thoughts back in. She'd have many choices for her hand. But what made him feel he should even be among those choices? No, he just needed to get through today, and then he would examine his feelings.

"Do you want to go inside the house?" he asked.

She stood and brushed the dirt off her pants. "No, not today. I'm weary."

"Captain can take us home and you can get some rest."

"What if I told you I want to dress this way for now on?" Her voice was hesitant and soft.

"I'd say we'd need to talk about it. You were fine being a young lady before Miss Cabot came, weren't you?"

She nodded. "It was easy with Dolly. She was showing me that being female wasn't bad at all. And of course, I see all the wives and their children. They are all so often smiling. Do you like children, Angus? You are well liked by the children, and I think you're fond of them, but do you want to have your own someday?"

He mounted Captain and held out his hand to help her up in front of him. "Perhaps someday."

CHAPTER SEVENTEEN

When they arrived home, Dolly pulled Julian into a hug first thing. "Come, let's get you fed. Went to pay respects to your father?" She didn't wait for an answer. "You've hardly had time to mourn him, what with everything going on here. Oh… Miss Cabot left if that makes you feel better."

Sighing in relief, Julian followed Dolly to the kitchen. "It does, but she was only doing what she was paid to do."

"It took everything inside me to keep from interfering." Dolly shook her head. "My poor tongue is sore from biting it."

Julian laughed. "Did she say why she was leaving?"

"Something about she was just wasting her time here. She also mentioned a sister. Teagan had Rafferty drive her. He heard about what Rafferty had said about your dress. It's his penance." Dolly laughed.

"Do you think I need to change my clothes?" Julian held her breath.

"I think tomorrow will be soon enough to put on a dress."

Tears filled Julian's eyes. "Dolly, I love you."

Dolly's eyes brightened with tears of her own. "And I love you, Julian."

Joy took the place of much of her sorrow. No matter what, this was her home now.

"I did learn a lot, but I have to confess it's a relief Miss Cabot is gone. She made me nervous, like each day was a daylong test. I hope—I mean maybe Angus won't find me so lacking now."

"Oh, sweetheart, I don't think he found you lacking. I believe he was trying to figure what the role of guardian entailed. He did it for you. He mentioned that you were shy and thought you might not feel confident being a girl. A lot of what Miss Cabot taught you is knowledge you can rely on. I don't think Angus or Miss Cabot knew you didn't have any desire to be a society wife." She patted Julian's cheek. "You are happiest when you are busy. I can just picture you with your own house and the joy you'll feel whether you are taking care of the house or the cattle. There is no reason you can't do both. You just need to find the right husband."

Was there really such a man out there? Because Dolly was right; doing both would be Julian's dream. If such a man existed, God would bring him into her life. Just as God would let her know when she was to marry. He'd be sure to send the right man to propose. If she only she had as much faith in herself as she did in God. Waiting might be hard, but wait she would.

Her heart felt lighter as she basked in God's love.

THE NEXT MORNING, Angus woke earlier than usual. He had a feeling something was wrong. Quickly he dressed and as soon as he was downstairs he ran into Teagan, who was seething and cussing, muttering about the payroll being missing.

"What do you mean the payroll money is gone?" Angus asked. His heart beat faster.

"I went to get it, and it's not there," Teagan said. His eyes glittered in anger. "Everyone on this ranch knows if they need money to ask for it."

"Let me look," Angus walked farther into the office and stopped at the oak desk. The money wasn't in the false bottom of the top desk drawer as it should be. He got on his knees and looked under the desk. Then he sat in the chair and emptied every drawer. Confusion enveloped him as he searched and then anger shrouded him.

"I don't understand. Who?" Angus asked Teagan.

"Julian's the only one of us who's new here." Teagan's eyes turned to ice. "Ask her what she knows."

"Seriously? She wouldn't—"

"So you say, but she's lied to us before…" Teagan said ominously.

A gasp from near the door drew Angus' attention. Face pale, Julian stepped into the room. "What are you saying?"

"Payroll's missing," Teagan told her, subjecting her to a speculative gaze.

"And you think I—"

"No," Angus broke in. "No one thinks—" He released a frustrated breath. "It's just, well, you have…" He couldn't choke out the word.

"Lied," supplied Teagan.

Crimson spots formed on Julian's cheeks. "It's true. I have lied to you, but I asked for God's forgiveness in the matter." She clutched and unclutched her skirt. "Angus?" Fear filled her eyes.

"Now wait a minute. We have no idea where the money

is, and making accusations isn't the way to find it," Angus practically growled, staring hard at his oldest brother.

Teagan's shoulders sagged in surrender, and he nodded. "You're right. I shouldn't have mentioned your name, Julian. I'm sorry. It's…been a stressful morning."

Julian nodded to Teagan and then looked to Angus. "Can I do anything?"

"No, honey. Why don't you help Dolly with breakfast?"

With fear still in her eyes, she gave him a small smile and then left.

Teagan ran his fingers through his hair. "Look, I'm sorry."

"It's fine. I'll see who is up and have them gather the brothers." Angus headed outside. He intercepted Fitzpatrick, who was on his way to the barn.

"Fitzpatrick, we need to have a meeting of brothers. Can you ask the others to meet us at the house as quickly as they can get there?" He paused, then figured why not? "The payroll is missing."

"What?" Fitzpatrick looked like he had a passel of questions. But instead of asking, he just said, "Sure thing, I'll have them shake a leg." Then he took off toward Quinn's house.

Angus took a deep breath and slowly let it out. If he didn't keep a cool head, he would go and hit Teagan in the mouth. How dare he suggest that Julian… Keeping a rein on his temper was getting harder, but he said a quick prayer and was able to do it with God's help.

Julian wouldn't have taken the money. She was a sweet woman, plus she wouldn't have had the nerve. She already felt uncomfortable with his family. This would just be too much. He hoped Teagan kept his mouth shut around everyone else about his initial suspect. They didn't need everyone suspecting Julian.

Angus poured the coffee while they waited on Sullivan.

The room was tense as the brothers sat at the kitchen table. Finally, Sullivan hurried in.

"Sorry." He grabbed a cup of coffee and sat down.

"The payroll money is missing. Angus and I searched the entire office. I'm hoping someone knows what's going on. Did any of you borrow the money?" Teagan asked as he glanced around the table, meeting each brother's eyes. Then he sighed as each shook his head.

"The only person I can think of is Julian. She's new here and she's lied to us before—" Teagan said.

A loud gasp came from the other side of the room. Angus knew who it was before he looked. Julian had one hand over her heart. Her eyes had gone wide, full of fright, as her face paled. She shook, but she didn't run.

"What are you saying? Teagan? You apologized for accusing me not a half hour ago. Why?" Her voice wobbled.

Teagan looked to be at a loss for words. He glanced at his coffee, then he raised his head and stared at her. "If you have the money, I'd like to have it back. I know things have been hard for you."

She quickly shook her head. Her hand dropped away from her heart as she wailed, "No!"

Angus stood, his chair making a loud noise as it scraped against the wooden floor. He hurried to her side and she wrapped her arms around his neck. She was his to protect. He lifted her into his arms and stepped outside to the front porch. He sat down and set her on his lap. His heart hurt as she burrowed against him.

"Why? Why would I take anything that didn't belong to me? You've given me so much I can never repay you for. Do I act ungrateful? Is there something about me that cries thief? I didn't do it." She sobbed against his chest.

To Teagan's credit, Angus knew he hadn't realized Julian was standing there when he had spoken. But as she sobbed against him now, his heart fractured for her. He'd wanted to bring her happiness and laughter, but he'd failed. Loud voices could be heard, including Gemma's.

Angus couldn't make out what she was saying, and then suddenly he no longer heard her. She probably left the room.

"I'm going to take you inside. Do you want to go to your room?" He needed to stick up for Julian.

"Yes," she said in a small, miserable voice.

"I know it wasn't you," Angus said. "I need to figure out what happened."

"It's simple," she said quietly. "It was Miss Cabot."

He frowned. Julian had a point. Miss Cabot had enjoyed free run of the house while she was there, and she had left before he'd been able to ask her to. He carried Julian inside, past his brothers, who all stopped talking, then up the stairs to her room, and set her on her bed. "I'll get everything straightened out, honey."

Angus stormed back to his brothers. He stood at the table and set his palms on it. After making sure he had eye contact with everyone, he started, "You should be ashamed for bandying about Julian's name. She pretended to be a boy as her pa taught her to protect herself from men. That does not make her a liar or a thief. She is the best person I know. Pick someone else to accuse!"

Dolly walked into the room. "My silver-plated brush and comb are gone. I had them wrapped and in my top drawer. My mother gave them to me before she died." She stared each brother down. "There's only one person who might have done this, and you all know who she is. So, what are you waiting for? Find Miss Cabot before she leaves town. And I want each of you to apologize to Julian as soon as you see her. That sweet girl has had enough heartbreak. She doesn't need y'all to gang up on her. I mean it; apologize by supper or don't step into this house again." She crossed her arms in front of herself.

The room was silent for a minute. The brothers all exchanged glances. Dolly could be bossy at times, but she'd never threatened them before.

"If I'm back before supper, Dolly, I will most certainly apologize, but right now I'm headed to town," Quinn said. "Fitzpatrick and Sullivan, ride with me."

Dolly nodded to Quinn.

Teagan put his head in his hands and sighed. "How stupid am I? Polite manners don't make a person honest. Miss Cabot had me fooled. I hope nothing else is missing." He stood and looked out the front window. "Angus, could you bring Julian into the office in a few minutes? I have much groveling to do."

"I'll bring her."

CHAPTER EIGHTEEN

*A*wkward would be the best term for her entire day. Teagan had offered to build her a house, which she declined. His eyes and hug conveyed how sorry he was.

It had been one apology after another, and Gemma was finally talking to everyone again. Dolly was probably relieved she didn't have to bar anyone from the house. She was overjoyed when Fitzpatrick handed the brush and comb set to her.

Julian sat on the sofa with Angus at her side. She tried to smile, but deep down she still ached.

"She stood right there in front of the general store with her many bags waiting for the coach to whisk her off to another town," Quinn explained. "Sullivan got the sheriff and before we knew it, there were at least three other families outraged and hollering at Miss Cabot. We have our money back." He held up a ring. "Gemma, I believe this belongs to you."

"Oh!" Gemma jumped up and took the ring from Quinn. She turned toward Teagan, who narrowed his eyes. "I thought I misplaced it. I would have told you eventually."

Teagan chuckled and shook his head. "I'm happy it's been recovered."

"Is everyone staying for supper?" Dolly inquired.

Quinn kissed her cheek. "I expect Heaven is waiting on me." He turned to Julian. "Again, I'm sorry about this morning."

Her cheeks heated once more. She nodded. She couldn't tell them everything was fine because it wasn't. Apologies were nice, but she was hurt, and she felt as though the ranch was no longer a place for her.

She ate little. Her stomach was as upset as she was. "Angus, could we take a walk after I wash the dishes?" She held her breath until he nodded.

"I'll help Dolly with the dishes. You two go ahead," Gemma offered.

Angus pulled Julian's chair out for her and led the way out of the house. He took her by the hand, and they strolled past the barn. "I want to show you something," he said.

She walked until he stopped. There wasn't much to see.

"You'll have to use your imagination, but this is where I'm building my house." He grinned.

She walked around imagining the views from the windows. "It's a pretty place, Angus. I wish you every prosperity."

"It sounds as though you won't be here when I build my house. I was going to wait until I found a wife, but I'd like us to leave the ranch house. A bit of distance would be good for you. I could feel how uneasy you were most of the day."

A ghost of a smile passed over her face. "It wouldn't be suitable for me to live with you alone."

"I don't care. I want to do right by you. I've already made too many mistakes where you're concerned, and I want you to have peace in your heart."

"That's sweet. When you get married, you'll bring your

wife to live with us?" She wouldn't be capable to stand seeing Angus setting up a household with another woman. He didn't feel the same about her. "I presume I should find a husband before you find a wife."

His smile withered and he stared into her eyes. If only she knew what he was pondering.

"I don't need a house to find peace," she told him. "Doing my chores and keeping busy will do it. It's the worst feeling when you know you didn't do something someone accuses you of. Thank you for standing with me."

He drew her into his arms and held her. She only allowed the comfort of his arms for a minute before she stepped back. "Thank you for showing me the spot your house will be. It's lovely here. But I'm tired now, Angus."

He took her hand in his again and walked her back.

Angus walked Julian to her room, appreciating the warmth of her hand in his. It startled him that he was hesitant to let her go. He told her good night, poured himself a cup of coffee, and headed out the front. He slouched in a chair with his legs crossed at the ankles. A lot had happened since he'd met Julian. He smiled, recalling the young impish boy. The Julian he knew now was guarded and didn't tell him what she was feeling. Was that the way of women, or was Julian pulling away from him bit by bit?

Part of it was his fault. He had aimed to be the best guardian ever, and that didn't include getting close to a female. What he felt for her was beyond guardian and ward. He needed to introduce her to the men in town. He grimaced. He wanted her, but it would have to be her choice. She wasn't in any shape to choose after all that went on with the missing money.

He'd find something they could do together tomorrow.

ANGUS GOT UP EARLY and saddled both Captain and Smokey. He tied them both in front of the ranch house. He stepped into the house, and the smell of coffee, bacon, and eggs hit him. His stomach rumbled.

"Angus, you're just in time," Julian told him with a big smile.

"You're full of sunshine this morning," he remarked as he took a plate from her.

"I'll get you coffee," she sputtered as her cheeks reddened. He watched her. She was more graceful than she'd been before the instructions. She was as beautiful as ever.

"Have you eaten?" he asked.

"Yes. I think I'll tend the garden today and then do a bit of laundry. What is your plan for the day?" She sounded excited about it. She was probably just glad she didn't have to do lessons anymore.

"I wanted to ask if you'd like to go horseback riding with me. I saddled Smokey for you."

Her eyes brightened. "Is this a joke or something?"

Dolly chuckled. "I think he's telling the truth, sweetheart."

Angus laughed. "Look outside. The horses are tied in front of the house. Think you can be ready to go when I'm done eating?"

She nodded and ran to her room. She came back with a big bonnet in her hand. "I made it myself. And before I put it on, I want you to know it's a poke bonnet and it's supposed to be big to keep the sun off my face." She put it on and secured the ribbon under her chin. He could barely see her face.

"Looks like it'll work good enough." He stood and held out his hand, and his heart raced when she grabbed it.

Tenderness filled him when he helped her into the saddle. "Hold tight."

She laughed. "It's a long way down."

When they were both ready, he led them in a slow walk toward the upper pastures. Captain wanted to go faster and then suddenly so did Smokey. They cantered to the pasture. Julian took her bonnet off at the last and the wind swirled through her hair. It was growing and he had a feeling it would be beautiful and thick when it finally fell over her shoulders.

"What are all the cowboys doing?" she asked.

"Deciding which of the cattle they will drive along the Chisholm Trail. It might be a good idea if we take a look at your herd and see if you want to sell any of them."

"I have a herd? But I thought…"

"You have a herd," he confirmed, smiling. "We found about fifty head on your ranch and… well, my brothers and I…*persuaded* the Fredericks to keep their end of the deal with your pa." He shrugged. "Leastways as far as the cattle were concerned."

She smiled. "I get to decide if I want to sell or not?"

"I thought we could make the decision together."

"Why would I want to sell them?" Her brow furrowed and lines formed on her forehead.

"Usually you want to sell the steers. You need a good bull to um, be with the cows so you can grow the herd. Cows who haven't calved are sold too. The concept is to have only the cattle you need in the winter because you have to keep them fed. You need to make sure you have sufficient hay for the winter. Also, this is how you make your money on a ranch."

"I see. What if I named a few of them and prefer to keep them?" She peered at him and he couldn't help but laugh.

"You named them?" He tried to stop laughing and hide his amusement, but it just made him laugh harder.

"You name your horses, don't you? You sell some of them." She raised her chin.

She was dismayed. He stopped being amused.

"I didn't mean to laugh. Most people will name the bull, but that's mostly it. It's fine, you can keep any you want. I have your herd over the hill. They are probably mixed in with all the others. We'll see what we can find."

He lightly pulled on the reins, turning Captain. Off they went, riding on the green grass that stretched across the hillside. Angus stopped at the top of the hill. "There they are."

"A beautiful sight, isn't it? It's so peaceful. There seems to be more than I thought."

"Your father did well buying the cattle. It was being swindled by the Fredericks that was his undoing. If he could have held on another year, he would have made a go of the ranch. I wish I could have gotten justice for you against the Fredricks about the land, but the sheriff wasn't interested, and a range war would have devastated both our ranches."

"I understand. If any of you were killed because of me... My pa would have been honored by your assessment of the ranch. It was a big chance to change from sharecropper to rancher. I was constantly afraid someone would find the money we saved."

"Sharecroppers don't make much, do they?"

"No, but we went without. We didn't require shoes or new clothes. We ate only what we grew or hunted. Most of what we grew went to the landowner, but we were able to sell some of our crops to the local people. I think people knew how badly we were treated and purchased from us. Once we realized we could indeed put away money, we decided to eat only two meals a day. I kept our clothes clean and mended. We had one mule, and that is how we traveled to Texas. The day we stepped onto our property was a proud day indeed. The only sadness was that Ma wasn't there to see it." She turned and settled her gaze on him. "I don't want a rich husband, Angus. I don't want to play a role or be a part of society. I'm just me, and being me isn't so bad. Someone will come along who likes me the way I am. God will send someone my way." She filled his heart with her words.

"You really aren't so bad," he teased. He craved to kiss her, but teasing was much more appropriate.

"And you are tolerable." She chuckled and suddenly stopped when their gazes collided.

Was that a flare of interest in her eyes? It seemed so much more, but he didn't dare hope. Instead, he grinned and kept his response light. "I know. Let's get back."

Nodding, she turned Smokey around and followed him. He slowed so they could ride side by side. "Aren't you going to put your bonnet on?"

"You don't like it? It makes it hard to see anywhere but straight. I like to have unrestricted sight. I'll wear my old hat when I ride from now on."

"I didn't say anything about not liking it. I just couldn't see much of your face while you had it on is all." The fullness of his heart bewildered him. If he were a betting man, he'd bet this feeling would lead to hurt.

CHAPTER NINETEEN

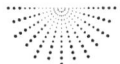

*J*ulian smiled at the image of herself in the mirror. The dress was lovely and appropriate for church. Butterflies filled her stomach. Dolly had helped her, but still the reaction of the others made her nervous.

She stood straight and tall, holding her head high as she took shorter steps. If she smiled would it be the sin of pride? She entered the sitting room and stood in the background while many Kavanaghs chased down their children. Meeting Dolly's gaze, Julian nodded at the housekeeper's smile of approval.

Angus came inside. "The wagons are ready." He turned and seemed to stare at her.

Was her dress not right? She started for her room. She was going to be sick. Angus touched her arm and she stopped.

"Come, I'll escort you to the wagon." He offered her his arm and she grabbed on. He was her anchor. They stepped outside and then down the porch steps. "You don't mind facing the back of the wagon as you go, do you?"

"No, that's fine."

He put his hands on her waist. "You look lovely. Green looks pretty on you. You're a fine, graceful woman, Julian."

Heat filled her and her heart seemed to flutter. Her face was on fire. Angus lifted her into the wagon as though she weighed nothing. "Thank you. I wanted your approval. Dolly helped me make the dress."

"She did it mostly herself. It looks beautiful on her," Dolly said proudly.

Julian's smile lasted until she entered the church on Angus' arm. She couldn't help but notice the stares and whispers. What had she done wrong this time? Was it her dress? Was she not walking properly? Was she lacking grace? Her hair was growing, but it had a long way to go before she'd call it pretty. Her heart raced and she needed to sit. Angus ushered to a pew and she moved until she was sitting next to Dolly. Angus and Dolly seemed not to have noticed. Perhaps it was her imagination.

She sat back and opened her Bible.

"I told you their definition of guardian differs vastly from ours. Why they act married, and that is just plain wrong," whispered a woman behind her.

Julian's heart dropped as she pretended she didn't hear the comment. The woman's words weren't Christian-like at all. Speaking ill of someone was wrong. Their information was wrong and she was implying something unseemly.

She'd worked hard, and it wasn't good enough. Taking a deep breath, she stared at the cross behind the pulpit. God loved her, and He knew she'd done nothing wrong. *God grant me the strength to forget such vicious words. Help me forgive and not be upset. Thank You for being with me. You are always there in my time of need.*

The Reverend stood at the pulpit and spoke.

Julian paid attention to every word. Her troubles seemed

to melt away, and she was less burdened by the time they sang the last hymn, Amazing Grace.

As Angus escorted her out of church, she walked with her shoulders back and her chin high. She hoped she was both graceful and elegant. She had God's love, and she also had the Kavanaghs to help her. No matter what anyone said, she was beyond grateful.

THAT WAS A DISASTER. Everyone had been whispering about his Julian. What right did they have to pass judgment on someone they didn't know? Couldn't they see how special she was? How vulnerable she could be? They didn't care if she was God fearing or not.

His poor brave girl. He admired how she pretended it didn't matter, but he'd been sitting right there and felt her stiffen as he heard the vicious gossip from behind them. There was no doubt in his mind she'd heard and it had cut her to the quick. Julian had gone right to her room after church and hadn't come back out. His first inclination was to leave her alone, but he didn't want her to hurt ever again.

He knocked and when she answered he walked inside. She was sitting on her bed in an everyday dress. Her eyes were red, and she looked up and tried to smile for him. He walked across the room and sat down next to her, taking her hand.

"Honey, I have something I want you to consider." He smiled as a feeling of tenderness came over him. "I think we should marry."

She stiffened and glanced away.

"I know you probably think my idea is crazy," he pressed on, "but Julian, I have deep feelings for you. The house I build could be for us to share as husband and wife. We could raise a family." His heart dropped at her silence. "I know it wasn't planned, but I'd be honored if you'd at least consider it."

Turning her head, she met his gaze. "I...I will, Angus. When do you need an answer?"

"Honey, this isn't a timed thing. I'd like to know sooner than later, but I want you to think it through. Don't marry me because of the gossip or to stay on the ranch. The ranch is your home no matter what." He leaned over and kissed her forehead. "No awkwardness between us, all right?"

She nodded, and he stood. He walked to the door and turned to gaze at her. Her brow was furrowed as though she was lost in thought. He went into the sitting room and watched his brothers with their wives and children.

It would be torture waiting for an answer.

WHAT HAD JUST HAPPENED? Angus had deep feelings for her? What did that even mean? Did he really care for her...in *that* way? She shook her head. No. He just didn't want her to feel sorry for herself. He didn't realize she had a grateful heart. How long would his feelings last? Would he forever be sorry if she said yes?

Julian stood and paced in her room. Did he think a new house made a difference to her? She'd loved him from the first, but the wall she built around her heart had been put up for a reason. They weren't suited. Or...perhaps they were. Everything was a jumble, and she trembled under the weight of the decision she had to make.

Lord, how do I make such a decision? For his sake, I must refuse. That would be the best way, wouldn't it? Lord, help me clear my mind. Do I listen to my head or my heart? Thank You for any guidance You give to me.

Quickly she washed her face and hurried to the kitchen

to help Dolly with supper. How was she supposed to not be awkward? Angus was watching her every time she looked that way. No more looking that way, she scolded herself. But the more she told herself not to look, the more she did.

"I know church was difficult," Dolly said. "I learned long ago not to pay any mind. They used to say things about the boys' father and me. We didn't have a relationship. We were two adults raising the children. It hurt that people said I wasn't a moral Christian woman. But through my faith in God and much prayer, my hurt went away."

Dolly stood close and held Julian's chin. "You have done nothing wrong. Have faith." Offering a cheery smile, she let go and went back to making biscuits.

Julian had so much to think about. She thought throughout supper, and still she didn't know. Angus would be a good, kind husband.

"Angus, can I have a word with you?" Her stomach churned.

"Yes. We can talk in the office." He put his hand on the small of her back as they walked. He led her to a chair and then closed the door. He sank down into the chair next to her. "What would you like to talk about?"

Shaking her head, she frowned. "There is a lot to talk about. You said you have deep feelings, but are they deep feelings of pity? What do you mean?"

A grimace flickered over his face. "I'm not the best at showing how I feel unless I'm angry, but with God's help I've been working on that. When you were 'the boy' in my eyes, I felt the love of a parent. I tried to hold on to that when I discovered your secret. After all, that would be the proper way to view you. I tried, really I did. I didn't want to love you like a man loves a woman. I didn't act on that love. I wanted to do right by you, but helping you find a husband is something I wouldn't be able to help you with." He pulled in a long breath. "Because I want to make you mine. I know you care for me, but it has to be more than that to get married."

He loved her? She couldn't allow herself to believe it, could she? Yet love was in his eyes, maybe...

"What about what people will say? You don't care what they think?" she asked, expressing her fear.

"If you love me back, then no, I don't care. That's why I want you to think about it. I don't want to take advantage of our situation. I don't want you to feel as though you have to marry me. I need someone who loves me heart and soul."

"Do you love me heart and soul?"

He nodded. "I do. Don't say anything. I really want you to think this all out." He stood and walked out of the office.

Oh my. Her heart was near bursting as a smile stretched across her face. She had butterflies in her stomach, but they were the splendid type of butterflies. If he hadn't told her to wait, he'd already know her answer, but she'd tell him tomorrow. Happiness soared through her.

Lord, he loves me. You knew already, but now I know too. I have been given so many blessings, Lord. I will work hard to be worthy of the blessings You have bestowed on me.

She kept to herself for the rest of the day and as night came, there was little sleep to be had. What if it was a mistake? Could she be a good wife?

Finally, as the sun rose, so did her confidence. Not everything she did was wrong. She was a capable, God-fearing woman with a good heart. She could do this. She would do this. Passing up happiness was not an option.

She dressed early and put the coffee on. Thoughts swirled in her head, but most of them were not of self-doubt. They were happy dreams of her future. Wandering out the back, all she spied seemed to be brighter than before. Was it because she loved and was loved? How glorious.

The door opened and closed behind her, and she knew it

was Angus. Her hands shook while she waited for him to come to her. She turned to him and smiled. "Yes, my answer is yes."

Angus picked her up and swung her around. Her heart beat faster and his joy was her joy. He set her down and kissed her. She'd never imagined his lips to be soft or his kiss to be soul searing.

"I was sure your answer would be no, and I wasn't sure how I'd handle it. You are a beautiful woman with a big heart. I intended on finding you a husband, but as each day passed, I recognized that I wanted to be that husband. I'd grown attached to the boy and it took me a while to actually see you. I was angry until I grasped that the qualities, I admired in the boy are the qualities you have as a woman. You are bright and easy to talk to. You have a love of learning. You are generous of heart and can ride a horse like you were born in the saddle. Best of all, you are mine."

EPILOGUE

*J*ulian asked the women for a moment alone. It had been a frenzy getting the wedding all planned and, in a few minutes, she was to walk to the love of her life. She touched the white lace on her white dress. It was so beautiful, and all the wives had helped to get it ready in a week.

Yesterday she visited her pa's grave, letting him know she would be married. He'd have approved, she just felt it. She walked into the cabin and on the mantel was a wedding photo of her parents. How had they afforded such an extravagance? She immediately placed it in her skirt pocket. She missed her ma, but the hole in her heart was being filled by Dolly and the wives. There was wonder in being embraced by the family. She'd walled her heart off to it all until Angus proposed.

She understood she was a capable woman who was not lacking. Especially as far as Angus was concerned. He committed to teach her more about ranching. She wept when he told her he wanted to teach her.

There was happiness in the world, and it took her a while

to discover it, but with God's help she did. She and Angus planned to reside in the ranch house until they built their own home and they discussed starting a family.

She'd been lonely growing up, and now she had more family than she knew what to do with. Moments alone were cherished. She decided not to sell her cattle, and Angus was fine with it. Wait until he finds out she named all fifty of them.

Claws peeked out from under the bed and then Paws and Jaws scampered out from under. "Who let you inside?" Julian smiled and shook her head.

It was time. Time to marry the man she cherished. Life was full of chapters it seemed, and she was starting a new one, a happy one, a blessed one.

After fixing her veil, she offered God praise and opened the door. She needed to walk down the aisle and marry the man who meant everything to her. Angus was her happily ever after.

THANK YOU

Thank you for taking the time to read Angus' story. The age of maturity in Texas in the late 1800s was really ten. Hard to believe. Rafferty's story will be on the Chisholm Trail as he tried to get the cattle to Kansas to sell. It was a trail fraught with danger but I suspect the Kavanaghs will be able to take on what ever comes.

ABOUT THE AUTHOR

Sexy Cowboys and the Women Who Love Them...
Finalist in the 2012 and 2015 RONE Awards.
Top Pick, Five Star Series from the Romance Review.
Kathleen Ball writes contemporary and historical western romance with great emotion and
memorable characters. Her books are award winners and have appeared on best sellers lists including: Amazon's Best Seller's List, All Romance Ebooks, Bookstrand, Desert Breeze Publishing and Secret Cravings Publishing Best Sellers list. She is the recipient of eight Editor's Choice Awards, and The Readers' Choice Award for Ryelee's Cowboy.
Winner of the Lear diamond award Best Historical Novel- Cinders' Bride
There's something about a cowboy

 facebook.com/kathleenballwesternromance
 twitter.com/kballauthor
 instagram.com/author_kathleenball

OTHER BOOKS BY KATHLEEN

Lasso Spring Series
Callie's Heart
Lone Star Joy
Stetson's Storm

Dawson Ranch Series
Texas Haven
Ryelee's Cowboy

Cowboy Season Series
Summer's Desire
Autumn's Hope
Winter's Embrace
Spring's Delight

Mail Order Brides of Texas
Cinder's Bride
Keegan's Bride
Shane's Bride
Tramp's Bride
Poor Boy's Christmas

Oregon Trail Dreamin'
We've Only Just Begun
A Lifetime to Share
A Love Worth Searching For

So Many Roads to Choose

The Settlers
Greg
Juan
Scarlett

Mail Order Brides of Spring Water
Tattered Hearts
Shattered Trust
Glory's Groom
Battered Soul

Romance on the Oregon Trail
Cora's Courage
Luella's Longing
Dawn's Destiny
Terra's Trial
Candle Glow and Mistletoe

The Kabvanagh Brothers
Teagan: Cowboy Strong
Quinn: Cowboy Risk
Brogan: Cowboy Pride
Sullivan: Cowboy Protector
Donnell: Cowboy Scrutiny
Murphy: Cowboy Deceived
Fitzpatrick: Cowboy Reluctant
Angus: Cowboy Bewildered
Rafferty: Cowboy Trail Boss

The Greatest Gift

Love So Deep

Luke's Fate

Whispered Love

Love Before Midnight

I'm Forever Yours

Finn's Fortune

Glory's Groom

Made in the USA
Las Vegas, NV
07 January 2021